Color Blind

An Interracial Christian Romance

Book One of the "Able to Love" Series

Michelle Lindo-Rice

Michelle Lindo-Rice
P.O. Box 495792
Port Charlotte, FL 33949

ISBN-13: 978-1499529616
ISBN-10: 1499529619

Table of Contents

Acknowledgements

I thank God for giving me the vision to write my first novella. His Holy Spirit guides me. I need him throughout the entire process.

Thanks to my sons, Eric Michael and Jordan Elijah, who let me follow my passion.

Thanks to author Rhonda McKnight. She's a true mentor. Thanks to Felicia Murrell. Her editing skills and work ethic is above par.

Thanks to Michelle Stimpson who wrote the book, 21 Days to Publishing. I used this guide to help me with the behind-the-scenes stuff to get this book published.

Thank you to everyone who will one-click this book. I hope you enjoy and receive a blessing.

Dedication

My sons, Eric and Jordan: May you both find real love without fear.

"There is no fear in love; but perfect love casts out all fear, because fear involves punishment, and the one who fears is not perfected in love." I John 4:18

Chapter One

Was that who he thought it was? Saul Sweeterman arched his wiry body over the steering wheel and peered through the windshield. His wiper blades sloshed away the fury of the pounding rain but it was difficult for him to see.

It was three o'clock on a Wednesday afternoon in May. Like clockwork, it was pouring rain. But even in the rain, he could see.

It was her.

He gazed at the passenger in the vehicle across the lane from him. Indeed, there sat his daughter, Cassandra Matthews, who hadn't spoken to him in three long, agonizing years.

Sitting at the intersection of Veterans Blvd and Atwater Ave., he was glad for the red traffic light because he'd been given a precious glimpse of his beloved Cassandra. Eyeing her black, no, African-American, husband, Kellan Matthews, resentment filled his heart. Saul's lips became as ugly as his feelings transforming into a harsh, angry line. Kellan was the reason he'd lost Cassandra.

Saul spotted a little head bouncing up and down in

the rear seat behind his daughter's seat. He tilted his head to get a better look. His granddaughter, Emily, was a beauty. There was no denying that. But, Saul's problem was that she was biracial, and Saul couldn't accept that. The races shouldn't mix. He didn't advocate slavery or apartheid, but Saul drew the line at interracial dating and marriage. It just shouldn't be done. That's what his parents had drilled into him from a child. It had been ingrained into his belief system. If pressed, he wouldn't be able to provide a legitimate argument as to why he held such a firm belief, but Saul didn't need one for something so intrinsically unnatural.

He had friends who were of a different race, but he'd never crossed that line. He hadn't felt the need to explain this to his daughter either. He had assumed that it was just understood. Saul had been wrong. He sighed. He'd made a fatal mistake when he hadn't spelled things out to his daughter.

"But your best friend, Uncle Marvin, is black," Cassandra protested the day she broke the news that she was pregnant and getting married to a black man. She pointed over to the picture frame displayed on the mantle.

Saul followed the direction of her finger and smiled with fondness. Marvin was a goofball and committed to the game. They'd spent hours bonding over basketball until an injury ended Marvin's chances in the NBA. Marvin didn't let that deter him, though. He kept on going. "Yes, but, that's because we played ball together. Marvin Alton was the exception. He married his own kind."

"You're prejudiced!" Cassandra screamed. She

clenched her fists and got right up in his face like she was ready to fight him. Like she wanted to hit him.

"Don't you fix your mouth to say those words," Saul said. "I'm not prejudiced—I just have my preferences. I'm being realistic. Your child will have a lot of issues to deal with. He or she will struggle with developing an identity."

"Are you listening to yourself?" Cassandra scoffed. She turned her head away from him blocking him from reading her face.

Saul remembered turning her head to face him. He looked into blue eyes so like his own, and touched her corn silk blond hair before saying, "Don't marry him, Cassandra. Don't have this baby."

She gasped and turned from him in one single motion. Shame crawled up his spine. Saul wasn't going to take his words back. He didn't believe in abortion, but this was a unique situation. This constituted an emergency.

"In this day and time you're asking me to be ashamed that I'm in love? When I told you about Kellan you sang his praises and encouraged me not to let such a promising young man, as you called him, slip away."

"Yes, but that was when I thought... I mean Kellan didn't sound like a..." Saul sputtered.

"A what? A *black* name?" Cassandra's eyebrows creased. She raised her hands to still his words. "Dad, please stop talking. You're going off every stereotype in the book and it shocks and saddens me. You're behaving like a dinosaur. I love Kellan and my baby, and we're going to get married."

With a patriarchal tone and a wide swoop of his hands, Saul dictated, "Well, I want no part of it. If you marry him, don't expect me to walk you down the aisle and smile and pretend I'm all right with you marrying someone you barely know—what's it been five months?"

Tears filled her eyes. Saul knew he'd hurt her, but he wasn't backing down.

Cassandra was just as stubborn. She walked out of his house, married Kellan and had her child without him. The only move Cassandra made was to send him a picture of Emily when she was born. Saul had the picture buried under some papers in his nightstand, but he never initiated contact.

The rain poured. Saul stared at his daughter, as the minutes crept by. She looked so much like Nora. He could hardly bear it. He shifted his eyes to look in the rearview mirror.

"What the?" He scrunched forward. Was he seeing right? There was a semi speeding in his direction. The moron was driving too fast for the slick roads. He wouldn't be able to brake in time. Saul's body clenched. This was an accident waiting to happen and the driver showed no signs of slowing down.

"Slow down! Slow down!"

The truck jumped the midline. Oh, no! He was heading straight for Cassandra's car. Saul's heart rate escalated. His palms sweated. He turned his body to get a good look behind him. Oh, boy, the truck wasn't going to stop. For a few tense seconds, Saul debated.

He jumped out of his truck. "Cassandra! Kellan!" he yelled. They were playing with Emily in the back seat.

Soaked, Saul scuttled towards his truck. There was only one way to circumvent what was coming. Saul knew what he had to do. He started the engine and slammed on the accelerator, praying his sturdy F-150 could take a hit. The truck driver must have finally caught on. Saul heard the sharp squeal of brakes. The semi began to spin on the slick road.

Saul continued driving. Cassandra and Kellan saw him at the same time. Their faces mirrored expressions of shock and horror as they looked up and saw the semi truck coming towards them. Saul registered their furious efforts to get Emily out of her car seat. "Get out the car," he roared. Kellan jumped into the rear seat and covered his daughter with his body.

A millisecond before impact, Saul swung his truck in front of their vehicle. The semi truck rear-ended him. Saul's F150 swung out into the ditch. He felt the crushing effect of steel against steel. Saul's body reeled as he narrowly missed being hurled into the street. Cassandra's car was now an easy target. The semi truck screeched to a halt as it slammed into their car. Saul heard screams and then a boom as glass shattered.

"Cassandra!" he wailed, willing his body to move, to go to his daughter, but a strong force pulled him slowly into blackness. As he succumbed, Saul heard a faint whisper in his ear, "Saul." The quiet voice soothed him and peace reigned as he drifted off. Then suddenly, all was silent and blessed quietness engulfed him.

Chapter Two

Six weeks later

Aniyah Hays knocked twice and then pushed the door open to Saul Sweeterman's room in the rehab wing of Fawcett Memorial. The lights were off and the curtains drawn. For a moment, she entertained the notion that Dracula waited to suck her blood dry. She grinned. Dismissing her fanciful thoughts, she slid the curtains back and turned on the lights.

"I didn't say come in." Saul Sweeterman snarled.

Now she knew why everyone on the floor called him Meanerman. She rushed to identify herself. "Mr. Meaner—er—Sweeterman. I'm Annie Hays, your physical therapist."

"I don't need a physical therapist," he answered. "I survived a punctured lung and a damaged spleen. I'm confident that in time, I'll be able to walk just fine. What I need to do is get out of here."

Annie counted to ten then employed de-escalation strategies, not wanting to rile his temper. With a light touch to his arm, she said, "Yes, in time, you will get out of here. But you're looking at at least another month or so before you can walk on that foot."

"Don't patronize me. I'm not four years old!" In a

swooping motion, he reacted, shrugging her hand off his arm. She wasn't prepared for his strength and found herself flung across the room. She crashed into the food tray.

He swung his head in her direction. "I—ah—I'm sorry. I didn't mean to do that." His gruff manner depicted a man who was uncomfortable with apologizing.

Annie didn't register his answer. Her mind was on two things. The first was that Saul Sweeterman had the most riveting pair of blue eyes she'd ever seen. The second was that they were unfocused and zoomed on a spot above her head. Sweeterman was blind. She'd read that when she reviewed his chart.

"Are you hurt? Ms. Hays, please answer me. I can't see for myself." He pointed out the obvious.

Annie nodded, before catching herself. She cleared her throat and found her voice. "Yes—I'm fine. No harm done."

So the bear had a gentle side. Interesting. Since he couldn't tell, she stared him down, taking in his blond hair and his imperial jawbone. He was super-hot. No one had mentioned that pertinent fact. And, those deep blue eyes reminded her of the clear Florida sky. Whew! She could stare into those orbs for days.

Then, he spoke. "You might as well leave and work on someone else because I'm not moving from this bed."

And, the Beast is back. Annie rolled her eyes but ignored him. She hummed, Tamela Mann's, "Take me to the King" and pulled the sheet back away from his leg. She wasn't going to chance a kick to her rib cage, so she notified him of her intentions. "Mr. Sweeterman, I'm going to examine your leg." Though she was petite, she had strong hands.

He jerked his foot in protest. "Don't touch me."

"I have to if I want to help you get back to normal. Dr. Pryor removed the cast, but you still have pins and screws in your leg. You've been immobile, but Dr. Pryor is thinking you're healing well enough to put you in a plastic walking cast." She made sure to keep her tone firm, so he'd know she meant business. She'd handled football players and basketball players. Annie wasn't about to let this one intimidate her.

"My left leg was broken in two places," he growled. "But I'm able to get myself to the bathroom."

"You shouldn't be out of bed, Mr. Sweeterman. You need to wait for someone to assist you. She lifted his leg with expert precision. "Your muscles are sore and tense. I'll work this out for you but you need to stay off your feet until Dr. Pryor says it's okay." She massaged both his legs.

He emitted a distinct masculine groan of pleasure, followed by a grunt of pain. Sympathy tore at her. "I'm sorry. It will feel better in a few minutes."

The angry line that was his lips curved a little. She saw a hint of a smile. "I can't wait to experience that feeling. It's been awhile."

She caught the double entendre. So, he was a flirt. She blushed and was surprised to find her heart beating faster. She cleared her throat and kept her tone professional. "I'm going to release the knots. It'll be uncomfortable for a minute, but then…" she trailed off, continuing her ministrations, until she heard a distinct release of breath.

"Ahh, I had no idea I was in pain. My legs feel like butter."

Annie had received this reaction from patients so many times in her career, that she'd been dubbed Magic Hands. With a pat on his leg, Annie said, "That's it for today. Tomorrow we work on getting you fitted for your cast and on your feet."

"Five more minutes please?" he begged.

Annie prided herself on her ability to remain detached. She had already stayed beyond the stipulated forty minutes. "A few more minutes, but then I have to go. I have other patients."

She hummed while she continued the massage before she said, "I'll be back on Wednesday to work with you again. In the meantime, please don't overextend your leg."

He nodded. "How many days will you be seeing me?"

"Twice a week."

"Oh." He sounded disappointed. She knew from the nurses that he hadn't had any visitors. Why should she care?

"I'm here in the hospital every day, though, so I'll swing by and check on you." She could've bitten her tongue. *Had she really uttered those words?* She wondered as she departed his room.

"You survived Meanerman," her best friend, nurse

Sari Noonan, said.

Annie smiled and winked. "He was sort of sweet," she mused, knowing she had a sappy look on her face.

Sari looked at her like she was crazy. "Sweet?

Annie grinned at the look on Sari's face. As she strolled towards the elevator, she admitted she was actually looking forward to seeing Saul again. As luck would have it, she ran into Sari on her next scheduled visit.

Sari shook her head when she saw where she was headed. "Good luck with him. He's in rare form. I told Dr. Pryor that I was through working with him. My job is to help and to heal not to be humiliated."

"Keep your head up," Annie reassured her friend. With a question in her eyes, she crept into the room. Her eyes scanned the tossed tray and the food contents splattered all across the room. Why had he done this? *Lord, please guide me and lead me.* She felt a tiny frisson of fear akin to Daniel entering the lion's den. Annie berated herself. He's a man, not a lion.

He could pass for one though. She placed a hand over her mouth with shock. Seeing his mane of hair all helter-skelter and his unshaven beard did sort of make him look like the king of the jungle.

"I can hear you breathing," he spat. "So identify yourself. I'm blind, not deaf."

His rudeness spurred her temper. She swooped all the contents off the floor and snatched one of the bed linens to clean the linoleum. She knew she could summon housekeeping, but Annie needed a moment to gather her wits or she was going to wring his neck with her bare hands.

"Are you going to answer me?" he hurled in her direction.

"Quit roaring at me," she snapped and went into the bathroom to wash her hands. She strode towards the door. She didn't have to put up with this rude behavior. Sari hadn't warned her enough. "I don't get paid enough to be insulted."

"No, Annie, come back! Please!" he roared pulling himself upright.

Her hand stilled. He called her Annie. She spun around. "Being a patient doesn't give you the right to be insufferable and mean."

"You're right," he hung his head. "That explains why I'm alone."

His puppy-dog face didn't fool her. "Quit the act. You're just trying to make me feel sorry for you."

"Is it working?" He gave her a lopsided grin.

Saul Sweeterman could be nice when he wanted. She chuckled and moved to undo his cast. She picked up his leg to give him a quick massage.

"So how come you're alone?" she asked, shifting the conversation into less dangerous territory.

He rested his head back against the pillow. "Well, I wasn't completely honest. I ran off all my buddies from the dealership with my bad attitude. No one's been to see me for weeks at my insistence," he said.

"So, your being alone is your own fault. You need to call your friends and apologize. You have a long road ahead and you can't do it by yourself."

He had the grace to blush. She watched the red splash across his cheeks and her hands stilled for a second. She made herself get back to work.

"I also have a daughter and a granddaughter," he chattered.

"What? You're not old enough to be a grandfather."

"I'm forty-three. Let me spare you the mental math by saying I was a young father," he drawled. His face depicted bliss from the work of her hands.

"Where do they live?" She switched to his other leg even though it didn't need massaging. "Make sure to keep exercising this leg. The other one you do with me."

He nodded and answered, "They're here in town."

"Really?" Her unspoken question hung in the air.

He must've been in need of a listening ear because Saul spilled. "I don't have a relationship with them because of my own stupidity. I didn't approve of the man she married and I allowed that to interfere with our relationship. I haven't even met my granddaughter. Her name is Emily."

She heard the regret in his tone but was surprised that he'd revealed so much of his business to a virtual stranger. "Why don't you call her?"

"Believe me, I would, if she'd let me. She's changed her number so I can't call her. Cassandra, that's her name—she blames me for her husband's death."

Chapter Three

Chanel No. 5. He'd recognize that scent anywhere.

"I didn't think you'd be back," Saul declared. In his mind, he pictured the willowy brunette with her body angled against the door. Macy Masters didn't stand. A top model, she was always striking a pose.

He didn't give her a chance to answer. "And, please don't tell me you have your secret agents lurking about," he added, referring to the dogged paparazzi men who popped up in the most unusual places.

"Don't worry, I know how to ditch those eels. It's just me, here. I value my privacy as much as you do," she replied, not hiding her contempt.

Saul nodded knowing how Macy detested the downside of having a recognizable face. He teased, "Are you hiding under sunglasses with your hair stuffed under a hat? I'm surprised no one recognized you."

Her laughter tickled his ears. "Don't laugh at my inspector Gadget getup. It has done me well. I didn't feel right leaving you here alone. If I have to come incognito, then so be it."

Saul was touched, but he didn't want to share his

feelings. So he threw out a useless taunt. "Didn't feel right leaving me alone while you spend my money?"

He heard a huge sigh and the clip-clop of her signature five-inch heels. Not that she needed them standing at five-eleven.

"Why is everything with us about money, Saul? Why does it have to be so cut and dry? I have money of my own. In fact, I have quadruple what you have so I don't need your pittance."

"Pittance? I've more than doubled my fortune since we met two years ago," Saul bragged. Her hand grazed his cheek and he lifted his chin in her direction. He inhaled. She smelled so good.

"I'm here because I love you and you're going to have to accept that," she whispered in his ear.

Deep down, he knew she told the truth. Macy was a beauty inside and out. He hated that he didn't return the sentiment. His accident had been the perfect excuse to push her away. He loved her but not in the way she craved.

When he didn't respond in kind, she groaned and stepped away. He knew he needed to say something to counteract her disappointment.

"I'm sorry, Macy. I've made no secret about the fact that while I have feelings for you, I don't feel the same."

"I know," she replied.

Her voice sounded hollow to his ears. He knew that tone. Saul wished he could see her face but he had seen the woebegone expression so many times that it was committed to memory.

Moments passed before Saul asked, "What's on your mind?"

"I'm thinking it's time I moved out," she said.

"If that's what you feel you need to do…" He felt the opposite of the words. Saul wanted to beg her not to leave. He needed her now more than ever. How was he going to find his way around? But he knew if he uttered the words, she would take it a different way, and read more into his request.

"Stubborn man. I only said that because I hoped you would admit you needed me."

"I do," he conceded. "But, not in the way you want." Even though he was on his face, he had to be honest with his feelings. He wasn't about to lead her on. "You knew this from the get go. I told you Nora was the love of my life. There is no replacing her."

"I'm not trying to replace your precious wife. But, frankly, she's dead and I'm here."

Her matter-of-fact statement jolted him. Saul knew he didn't want to talk anymore. "I think you should leave," he bit out.

"I didn't come to upset you, although lately that's all I seem to do." He heard movements. She must be getting ready to leave. "I'll be out of town on a modeling job. I tried to get out of it but that's business for you. Signed contract and all. If you call me with your discharge date, I'll make sure I'm here."

"I understand. I'll let you know when I know for sure," Saul interjected, hoping his voice didn't show the relief he felt. He puckered his lips and waited. Her lips touched his and they shared a brief kiss. As usual, it was pleasant but something was missing.

Was he still hooked on his wife?

Saul debated that question for hours after she left. He thought about Nora Sweeterman, the love of his life. High school sweethearts, they had chosen to marry after graduation, much to their parents chagrin. But, Saul had known she was the one.

Unfortunately, Nora died of an asthma attack when Cassandra was eight years old. Since then, he'd dated here and there. Macy had been his first real attempt at a relationship since Nora's passing.

Macy was smart, beautiful and successful. She wanted more than Saul had to give. She wanted his love. Saul had nothing against falling in love. He just wasn't sure he could.

Chapter Four

"Mr. Sweeterman?"

He smiled, recognizing Annie's voice. "I'm sorry I must have drifted off. And, it's Saul," he insisted.

"Are you up to our session? I could reschedule?"

Hearing the question in her voice, he pushed himself up to a sitting position. "No, don't reschedule. I…" He stopped. There was no way he was admitting that she was the high point of his hospital stay. Her presence was calming.

He heard a light chuckle before Annie got started. Five minutes passed as he reveled in the relief her hands brought. "You're quiet tonight."

"It's actually early evening," she corrected. "I have a lot on my mind."

"Care to share?"

"I shouldn't." He heard the hesitation in her tone. Normally, he'd respect that and mind his business but he'd gotten used to her humming. Something was bothering Annie and it concerned him.

"My roommate's getting married in a few months. I

was thinking that instead of leasing another apartment, I'd buy a home. But, I also need a new car, so…"

"I see." Saul grimaced while she kneaded the knots in his legs. He had no idea he was so tense. Once she finished, he said, "Go with the home. It's a lifetime investment. You can use your home to purchase a car. I know someone who can give you a good deal on a car when you're ready," he smiled.

She laughed, "Thanks, but I couldn't do that."

"If I could see, I'd hand you my business card. I'll dictate my information to you instead."

Her hands stilled.

Saul paused. This was the first time he'd mentioned his blindness without the usual flash of temper.

"I know it must be difficult losing your sight," Annie stated.

"That's an understatement," he agreed, raking his hands through his hair. "Every morning I wake up and I forget that I can't see anything but shadows. Then I open my eyes and it hits me all over again."

"Mr. Sweeterman—I mean, Saul—I know what I'm about to say sounds trite, but you're alive. You shattered your tibia and fibula bones when you collided with that semi. You hit your head hard during the collision, but thankfully, God spared your life."

"Yes, I should be grateful to be alive," he interjected, "I know all that. But, losing my sight is a huge challenge. It's overwhelming. I didn't realize how much I used it until I lost it. Nothing is the same."

She tapped his side and helped him shift positions.

"Have you thought of seeing a therapist?"

Macy had been nagging him to see a professional. Whenever she brought it up, he usually had a smart rebuff. He relayed the same sentiment to Annie in gentler terms. "Unless talking to one will restore my sight, I'll pass."

She giggled at his sarcasm. "There are emotional and psychological effects that a therapist can help you work through."

He relaxed. "You're all the therapy I need at the moment. Thanks."

She didn't push. "Think about it."

By now, Saul knew her routine. She was almost finished. He realized he didn't want her to go just yet. He had to think of something to stall her leaving. "Can you read to me?"

"What do you want me to read?"

He shrugged; glad to hear the shuffling of pages.

"I'll read Psalm 91."

Saul nodded. She could've been reading the telephone book and he wouldn't have cared. With a sigh, he adjusted his pillow to listen to her melodious voice.

Chapter Five

"Saul Sweeterman is feeding you lies," Sari stated as she dug into her Santa Fe salad at Chili's.

"What do you mean?" Annie asked, taking a sip of her lemonade.

"He's not alone. I think he has a girlfriend."

Her heart skipped a beat but Annie strove for nonchalance. No way was she letting on that she even cared. "Why do you say that?" she ducked her head to stab her fork into her salad.

"Because I overheard the nurses saying that he had a lady friend come sit with him and this woman has called more than once to check on him."

Annie took a careful bite but she shrugged. "Okay? And, you're telling me this because…"

Sari curled her lips. "This is me you're talking to, your best friend since college. I know when you like someone."

Annie and Sari had met as classmates in college in their hometown of Jacksonville. They'd had an instant connection and their friendship had remained intact through Annie's broken engagement and Sari's marriage, divorce and the drowning of her only child, Lucas. Sari had found peace and a new boyfriend when she'd given her life to Christ.

"I've gotten to know Saul a little bit over the past couple of weeks, but that's all there is to it," Annie assured her, before taking a bite of the quesadilla she ordered as an appetizer to go along with her salad. She wasn't ready to admit to herself or her best friend how much she looked forward to her visits with Saul.

"Well, he has a mystery woman in his life," Sari reiterated. "What you need to do is take Ahmad up on his offer to set you up."

She spoke loud enough to attract the attention of an elderly couple behind them. Annie could've sunk into the floor. She gestured to Sari to lower her voice.

"I don't need your boyfriend pimping me out to his friends," Annie whispered. Ahmad Givens was a pediatrician with offices near them on Caring Way. Sari had met him online and relocated to Port Charlotte from Jacksonville to be closer to him. Annie followed her friend.

When Sari became saved, Annie had been her first convert. Ahmad was her second.

"Dr. Baxter Reynolds doesn't need a pimp," Sari bristled. "He's a man of God and all the ladies at church are swooning over him."

"Tell Ahmad no thanks. I don't need a snaggletooth physician any time soon." Dr. Reynolds was extremely handsome but his jagged front teeth were distracting. When she met him briefly before, all Annie could think was, *with all his money, why can't he fix his teeth?*

Sari reached for a tortilla chip and threw it at her in jest. "God's going to get you for that."

"I know you and Ahmad mean well, but I'm good. Jesus is my boyfriend for now."

"Hmmm."

"What does hmmm mean?"

"Don't throw Jesus in the mix. For one thing, since we call God, Father, that makes Jesus our brother so He can't be anybody's boyfriend." She waved her fork around in circles. "You're not interested because of Saul. Normally, you would've given someone like Baxter a chance, but you're all caught up with Meanerman."

Sari had a point. Annie sighed. "I do like Saul. Something about him pulls at me."

"I'm sure it has nothing to do with the fact that he's fine as ever," she teased.

"That doesn't hurt," Annie confessed with a wide grin. "But, I feel a connection."

"Well before there's any connecting going on, you make sure you ask him about a woman in his life."

Annie didn't want to dwell on that possibility. "He does have a daughter and a granddaughter."

Sari leaned closer. "He comes with baggage?"

She bit her lip. "Not really. They're estranged."

Her friend's eyes popped wide with curiosity. "Why doesn't he have a relationship with his own child?"

"I don't know. I didn't ask. He confessed that he hasn't spoken to her in a few years. Her name's Cassandra—and get this, she was involved in the accident as well. She was admitted to the hospital but was released either the same day or the next day." Annie waved her hand, dismissively, "I forget which…"

Annie cracked up as Sari was salivating from the tidbit of gossip. She wouldn't divulge that she had a secret motive for sharing Saul's personal information.

"You should've asked. I'm concerned. A man who isn't in his child's life is a warning sign. Don't you hear the warning bells?"

Annie gulped. Her friend was poking holes into her happy balloon. "That is strange, but from what I know of Saul, he must have a good reason."

Sari gave her a pointed look. "You're farther gone than I realized. You're defending him."

"I'm not…" Annie stopped, realizing she was doing just that. She was defending a man she barely knew. Her heart rate increased.

Sari grabbed her bag to pull out her iPhone. "What's her name again? I want to program it in my phone. I've got to look her up so we can see what she looks like."

Mission accomplished. Annie relaxed into her seat to finish her meal. If her plan worked, she would have what she needed to help Saul reunite with his daughter.

That was her first move.

Then she would find out about this mystery woman.

Chapter Six

Seven digits.

These numbers were all it took to change Saul's life and she had them written on a small piece of paper, between her fingertips. Annie had looked at the paper so many times that she had the number memorized. Should she call?

She came from a close-knit family, so Saul's estrangement with this daughter tore at her heart. Sari had been more than willing to help her play the heroine. A few clicks were all it took for Annie to have what she needed. According to the screen, Cassandra had been admitted, treated and released the next day. Her contact information was there for all to see.

Now all Annie had to do was call, or give Saul the number to call. Unsure, she paced outside his hospital room while she debated. "He needs this," she decided, and entered his room.

"Saul, I have it," she whispered looking towards the door. She knew it was her overactive imagination at work, but Annie felt guilty about what she'd made Sari do. Any moment, she expected to see her friend walking out the building with two beefy security guards trailing behind for breaking patient confidentiality.

"What do you have?" he asked.

"Your daughter's number," she supplied, gripping the small paper with sweaty palms.

"How did you get it?"

"I asked a friend to look her up," she replied. No way was she telling how curious about him they'd been.

He creased his brows. "Can you do that?" he asked.

Knowing he was right to question her made her defensive. "Do you want it or not?"

"Uh—I can't see it."

Oh yeah. She hadn't thought of that. Some people weren't cut out for crime. Annie was sweating cats, dogs and elephants. "I'll program it in your phone. Then you can use your voice dialing to call her."

Saul was dressed in street clothes. Annie had to admit, he looked good in those dark, blue jeans. It took effort, but she willed her eyes up to his face, glad he couldn't see her ogling him. Saul pushed his hand into his pocket and retrieved his phone. He held it out to her.

Their hands connected. Magnetized energy discharged between them catching her by surprise.

"Uh—thanks," he said.

Not missing the lowered decibels in his voice, Annie withdrew her hand as if she'd been stung. She cleared her throat. "It's no problem. I just want you and your daughter reunited." She took the phone out of his hand.

Strong hands snatched her hand back into his and wouldn't release her. "I want you to come with me."

"Say what?"

"I didn't mean that the way it sounded. I meant I want to hire you," he said. "When I'm discharged, I want you as my personal therapist—full-time. Name your price."

"I don't know about that. I love working here." She removed her hand from his, and clasped her hands together to compensate for the sudden lack of warmth.

He wasn't going to give up that easy. "I still have a week before I leave, so think on it."

She nodded before she remembered to answer. "Okay, I'll give your offer serious consideration but you have to promise to change. You have to be nice to the staff, especially my friend, Sari."

He bunched his lips at her admonition. "I guess I haven't been the easiest of persons to deal with," he acknowledged.

"No, you haven't." Gently, she said, "I know you have a long road ahead but God won't give you more than you can bear."

"This is the second time you've mentioned God. Don't tell me you're a Bible thumper," he snorted.

Annie took umbrage at his condescending tone. "Yes, I'm a Christian, and don't judge me because you don't know anything about me. To be honest, you need some God in you right about now."

Saul held his hands up in a gesture of surrender. "Okay, take it easy. I meant no harm, I promise. Boy, you're a feisty one aren't you?"

"Yes, but only with my friends. I'm usually more professional with my clients," she chuckled. "I don't even know how you get to me."

"Will you come work for me? My house is large enough to accommodate you."

"I don't think that's a good idea. Plus, what about your girlfriend?" She asked the question uppermost in her mind. "I don't think any woman will be all right with another young woman under her roof, even if it is business."

"I'm a grown man, Annie, and it's my house. You said yourself that I would need around the clock care. I want you and my girlfriend is not the jealous type. She'll like you and she'll be glad to have you there."

She didn't argue with his logic, but she knew women. Nevertheless, she didn't press the issue. Though this wasn't the first time a client had wanted to contract her for private services, this was the first time; she was tempted to say yes. "I'll pray on it," Annie promised. "Don't you feel apprehensive about inviting a stranger into your home? I could rob you blind." She paused a beat. "Er, poor choice of words."

"You could," he answered, matter-of-factly. "But I trust you."

She pulled her hand away from his. "You just met me. How can you trust me already?"

"How long does it take?"

****

"You can't seriously be considering his offer?" Sari

said. She curled her legs under her and settled into the couch at their apartment.

Annie bit her bottom lip. "I'm thinking about it. It's good money. Saul Sweeterman owns several car dealerships so it's not like he can't pay me."

Sari gave her a look. "Girl, please. Who you fooling? You don't care about money, you never have. If you did, you would have married Cornell Adams and been the wife of a Miami Dolphins linebacker. You like Saul Sweeterman. That's why you want to go. And, have you missed the significance of his name?"

"No, I haven't missed the fact that his namesake in the Bible also lost his vision. But, he's alone. I feel sorry for him. Saul needs my help, even if he doesn't know it."

"Annie, he has a girlfriend. He's not alone. You're the best physical therapist on our floor. If I thought this was all business, I would be jumping for joy." She swept her hands across the small living area. "But, he's a man and you're a single woman who is attracted to him. What you think is going to happen with you two all by your lonesome in his mansion?"

"First of all, I don't think he lives in a mansion. Secondly, I'm grown. I can handle attraction. I—I want to go. I feel led to." She didn't add that she didn't think she could bear not seeing him. It would make her seem desperate.

Sari waved her hand in annoyance. "He lives in Boca Grande—home of the mansions, and don't even bring the Holy Spirit into this discussion. I think it's a different spirit sending you under that man's roof." She reached over to the end table and picked up her cold glass of lemonade.

"I'm not leaving the Holy Spirit behind," Annie said. "Wherever I go, He goes. He won't steer me wrong. I'll be all right."

Sari shrugged. "It sounds like you've made your decision."

Annie crooked her head. She didn't respond. She let her eyes say what words didn't. Yes, she had.

Chapter Seven

"Thanks for the ride, Greg," Saul said. He lowered his head as he exited the luxury car. He used the cane in his hand to help him navigate. He'd had a crash course before leaving the hospital. He knew he needed an orientation and mobility specialist. Saul hated the contraption, but he had to use it or risk losing one of his toes. He'd bumped his feet and hit his shins too many times to count, so the cane stayed.

"It's so good to be home." It had been seven weeks since his accident and it was now the middle of July. When Saul first left the hospital, the heat was the first thing that greeted him. He welcomed the feel of the oppressive sun and now wished he hadn't been so adamant to stay inside. He'd forgotten what he was missing.

"Not a problem, boss," Greg Holmes said. "Business hasn't suffered from your absence. If anything, since the news of your—ugh, demise—we've been booming. We can't keep cars on the lot, and the special orders have us working overtime."

Saul was impressed. His neighbor's here at Boca Grande were some of his best customers. He supposed this was their way of 'helping.' Little did they know he would've appreciated a visit or a phone call, instead of them fattening his bank account.

If it weren't for Annie's visits, he would've gone

insane. For the umpteenth time, he wished he could see her. All he had to go by was her beautiful spirit and her voice. Her voice soothed him, as she sat with him and read the Bible or the Charlotte Sun. Saul had come to admire her wit and her overall optimism in life. A couple of times, she'd prayed for him.

Annie was scheduled to arrive in three days and Macy was due in from Milan in a couple of hours. He was sure he could manage until then. For years, it had been just him and Cassandra, after his wife died of asthma. Then when Saul met Macy he attempted to move on, but his heart wasn't complying.

Thinking of his daughter made him sigh. He finally called her a week ago and left a message. As far as Saul was concerned, it was now in her hands. He wasn't about to beg his own offspring to have a relationship with him. Not for one minute would he admit that his heart hurt from her rejection.

By the time Saul returned from his thoughts on Cassandra, Greg had guided him inside his home. The crisp air conditioning and the smell of lemons told him that his cleaning lady had been by. He swooped the cane from side to side and walked with careful movements navigating his way into his living area with Greg's help.

Saul hated relying on anyone, but he was grateful that Greg had been willing to escort him home.

"Are you sure you'll be okay?"

Saul heard the worry in his friend's voice. "Yes, I'll be fine. Macy's coming in tonight and my therapist will here on Thursday. It's only three hours, I'm sure I can manage until then." Saul injected more bravado than he actually felt.

"Will you ever see again?"

Greg's question hit him in the core. It was something he thought about a gazillion times per day. "I don't know. The ophthalmologist told me that my eyes weren't physically damaged. Everything is working, as it should. He doesn't have a clue why I can't see. He even intimated that I was choosing not to see." Saul laughed with self-deprecation. "Yeah, like I would really choose to hit my shin at least three times a day."

"When a doctor speaks like that, only God can help you," Greg said.

Greg left after that, but his words lingered.

God. Saul rubbed his chin. He'd never given much thought to the Man upstairs so if God was the only Person who could help him, then he was in serious trouble. He only went to church for weddings and funerals so why would God waste time on someone like him?

He sighed. His own daughter wanted nothing to do with him.

Holding one hand out in front of him, Saul used the cane in his other hand to pick his way around his living area. With cautious steps, he located the guest suite in the back of the house. His master was upstairs, but he knew he couldn't handle the stairs. Somewhere deep inside Saul knew he'd been wrong to cut Cassandra out of his life. However, he was too stubborn admit it.

He felt a huge sense of accomplishment when his cane tapped against what must the bed. When his hand pressed into the soft mattress, Saul exhaled and turned to sit on the bed.

Saul had no idea what time it was or how long he sat there. But, he got tired of the croaking frogs and those noisy grasshoppers. Reality sunk in, he was blind and alone in this big house. He thought he'd been alone in the hospital, but in actuality, someone was always coming into his room.

Saul swallowed and tapped his cane on the floor just to make some noise. It echoed through the room. He didn't like being here by himself. He was used to being on his own, but that was before he was blind. He dug his cell phone out of his jeans to call Cassandra.

Again, he got her voicemail. He hung up without leaving her a message.

He tossed the phone across his bed. It landed with a thud on the floor. He groaned. Now, how was he going to find it? His leg prevented him from getting on his knees.

Oh, how he wished he'd listened to Annie when she advised him to work with a vision teacher or orientation and mobility specialist. The cane had been his only concession. Saul refused the visiting nurse services provision as well.

His stomach growled. In his mind, he pictured his refrigerator well stocked with containers of food and stood. It took him twenty minutes to reach the kitchen. He rubbed his nose. His house was now a war zone. Saul opened the door and reached inside. He felt empty space before his hands encountered something cold.

It was a bottle, which he hoped contained water. Other than that, his fridge felt bare. He'd neglected to have his food prepared and delivered. He could find his way around a kitchen and had never worried about simple things like eating—not when he could afford anything under the sun. For the first time in his life, Saul was scared. His life as he knew it was over. He was helpless.

He untwisted the cap and guzzled the water like it was fine wine. Within seconds, he held the empty plastic container in his hands. Suddenly enraged, he crushed it and threw it from him. He was hungry, angry, and now he had to pee.

"Argh!!!" he screamed. "Help me!" His voice boomed into the empty space.

Unfortunately, his nearest neighbor was a mile away. His reclusive home was... reclusive. *What did I do to deserve this?* In a fit of unquenchable rage, he swung his fists. Heedless to the clatter, clanging, and crashing, he destroyed whatever he touched.

When there was nothing left that he could feel, Saul sunk to the floor heaving from his exertion. He did something he hadn't done since Nora's passing. Saul cried and cried and then he cried some more. Definitely not his most manly moment, but he needed the release.

An interminable amount of time passed before his tears subsided. Saul looked upwards and croaked, "Macy, where are you?" On cue, he heard the house line ring. He knew it was on the counter and gripped the cabinet to hoist himself to his feet. The shrill sound of the telephone set him on edge. He fumbled for the cordless and answered, glad it hadn't gone to voicemail.

"Saul, I'm stuck in Fort Lauderdale. I caught a bug and my stomach's acting up. I had to check into a hotel.

I don't want to take a chance and drive through Alligator Alley feeling this unsettled." Macy stated. He heard the despondency in her tone but at the moment he was more concerned with himself.

He gulped to keep from yelling that he needed her here right now. "Take care of yourself. I'll manage. It's just one night."

"Do you want me to call Linda?" she asked, referring to Linda Clemente, his housekeeper.

"Her husband sprained his leg so she's out of commission." Saul tried to hold his dejection, but he couldn't contain the sigh.

"You know what? I'll take a chance. I'll try to come."

He really wanted to tell her to come but her voice sounded pained. "No. Stay where you are. Manny is due to trim the lawn in the morning. I'll holler out for help when he comes."

Somewhat mollified, Macy rushed off saying the bathroom was calling. Reluctant, Saul pressed the end button.

No Macy.

No Cassandra.

Just him.

What was he going to do?

Chapter Eight

Annie's favorite novel of all time was Jane Eyre. As a teen, she'd spent countless hours reading and re-reading the story. Any movie that was made about Jane Eyre, she watched. The latest one starring Michael Fassbender and Mia Wa—Annie always forgot her name - was her favorite.

Well, fiction had now come to life for it seemed Annie had met her own Mr. Rochester. In Charlotte Bronte's novel, Jane Eyre had been hired to take care of Mr. Rochester's ward when they fell in love. She knew it was silly but it was like she heard him calling her. "Annie! Annie!"

It was now 7:02 p.m. on the clock. Her usual routine included laundry and a stint in front of the television to catch up on *Scandal,* which she kept in her DVR. Instead, she was pushing her feet into her sneakers and searching for her keys.

Saul had assured her that his girlfriend was coming to take care of him. She didn't want to interrupt what must be a lover's reunion, but he hadn't answered her phone calls. Something within her wouldn't settle until she'd checked on him. If she looked stupid, then so be it. It wouldn't be the first or last time.

Annie drove the forty-minute drive to Saul's home. He'd given her simple directions, told her where he kept the spare key and even entrusted her with his alarm code. Annie's eyes widened. She took a snapshot on her iPhone. Sari was wrong. He lived in a mausoleum, not a mansion. She parked her plain old Camry next to a Lexus and a Corvette and walked around the back of the house to retrieve the key from under the mat.

She heard wails coming from inside and raced to the front to unlock the door. Her heart hammered as she moved towards the sound, unsure of what she might see.

She saw the open refrigerator door—correction, the empty, open refrigerator door. With tentative steps, she approached. She closed the door and looked around in shock. The counters were bare. Broken glass was everywhere. In the midst of all that squalor sat Saul—looking lost and scared.

Her feet crunched on the broken glass.

His head swung upwards, "Annie, is that you? How did you know to come?"

Saul spoke as if he didn't expect an answer, almost as if he really didn't believe she was there.

"Yes, it's me. I don't know why I came. I know from experience how difficult the first night home can be for many patients and I decided to check on you," she said. Yeah right. She wasn't crazy enough to share her Jane Eyre moment.

"You're here? I've never been so happy to hear

someone's voice in all my life," He exaggerated as he reached for her.

Annie's heart skipped a beat. She bent to cup his hand into hers understanding his need to make human contact. When their hands joined, it felt right. She looked into his unseeing eyes and said, "I'm here." *And, I'm not going anywhere,* she added to herself.

***

"What's Saul Sweeterman doing here?" Sari whispered, pointing to the large man asleep on their couch. She slurred his name as if she were referencing a contagious disease.

Annie paused from packing the reusable grocery bag and greeted her friend with a sheepish smile. Sari had just ended her shift. Annie replied, "I gave him his pain meds which knocked him out. Don't worry, he's not staying. I just needed to grab my clothes and some food to hold us over until tomorrow."

Sari put her hands on her hips and looked at Annie as if she were crazy. "Are you listening to yourself? When's the wedding? Because at the rate you're going, you two will be married in a month."

"I know this all seems crazy, but I'm not cuckoo," she defended. "And he has a girlfriend."

Saul stirred on the couch, but didn't awaken. Annie placed a finger over her lips and tilted her head towards her bedroom. Sari nodded and stomped inside.

"I promise you that I'm in my right mind," Annie began again, "But, I'm going with the flow and helping someone in need."

"He's rich and wants for nothing in this world. What could he possibly need?"

"A friend," Annie supplied. "He needs one of those."

Sari grunted. She marched over to the nightstand to get a post-it note and a pen. "Write the address here and all of his phone numbers. I want to be sure that if my black friend goes missing, I know where to send the police."

Annie popped her hand over her mouth before saying, "Oh my goodness, what do you think he's going to do to me? I assure you, I'm safe with him. "

"I watch *Criminal Minds*... I'm just saying be careful. It's always the handsome ones." When she pulled out her cell phone and left the room, Annie trailed behind.

She watched with something akin to horror as Sari snapped a few pictures of him before shoving her phone in her pocket. She patted her pants, "Evidence."

Annie chuckled at her friend's paranoia. "Whatever." She couldn't expect Sari to understand something she herself didn't understand. Her attraction to Saul Sweeterman had been unexpected, but...oddly welcomed. She was glad that she found Saul when she had. After she'd helped him to the restroom, Annie cleaned up the mess in the kitchen. He had been so vulnerable and clinging to her. He cried in her arms. She used that opportunity to pray for him.

Annie was glad that Saul finally listened to her and would be consulting with a vision teacher. He needed to learn how to adapt to living without his sight. She sighed. What he really needed was a psychiatrist—and

God.

Her eyes gravitated towards his sleeping frame. Though he'd been grateful for her prayers, Annie's heart flip-flopped when he asked, "What does God want with me?"

How she wished she'd used the moment to minister to him. Instead, overcome with emotion, she'd done nothing, but hold him. "I'll do better, Lord. Next time I get the chance, I'll share more of You," she whispered.

Her next time was sooner than she anticipated.

It was Wednesday night, two days since she'd taken on her live-in assignment. Annie felt at peace in Saul's home. He'd moved into the bedroom downstairs and had offered her his master suite.

"I can't take your room," she protested.

"I insist," Saul returned. "It's the best room in the house. You'll love the view of the water."

"Thanks for the offer, but I'll move into one of the other two rooms upstairs. You mentioned a girlfriend. I can't see any woman being okay with that."

"Don't worry about my girlfriend. The room is yours to use. She caught a bad bug. I'll explain when she gets here, tomorrow."

She switched subjects. "The vision teacher is coming tomorrow to work with you and then we'll have our session."

He nodded. Annie heard him clear his throat. "I never thanked you for the other night, for being there. I don't know how you knew to come, but I would've fallen apart if it weren't for you."

Annie appreciated his sincere words. "I would've done it for anyone," she demurred, knowing she wasn't being honest with herself. She excused herself and retreated to her room after that.

She settled into the silk sheets and couldn't help stirring at the thought of Saul Sweeterman lying here. Her senses awakened. She was a woman with needs and it'd been awhile. She exhaled. "Lord, keep me true and my actions pure." She inhaled his woodsy scent that lingered in the air. This wasn't a good idea. Sari was right. Why had she moved in with him?

He looked like a Greek Adonis. Attraction between a man and woman was powerful. Would she be able to resist his charms? She groaned. This was torture. Images of him in this bed, in his shower, touching where she touched plagued her mind.

"Ugh," she jumped up. "I can't sleep." She turned the television on but with all the channels, nothing captured her interest. Her mind was filled with the blue-eyed hottie downstairs.

Giving into impulse, she donned a robe and wandered through the kitchen until she was standing outside his door. She pressed her ear to his door. She heard wails and moans coming through the door. Annie put her hand on the knob to enter before she stopped herself.

She was the hired help. Going into his room was a no-no. There was the big question of what was she doing stalking him outside his bedroom door. She heard another muffled scream and her instincts took over for her.

She was a professional and recognized

posttraumatic stress disorder when she heard it. He was reliving the crash.

"No! No!" he screamed.

Decision made, she pushed open his door. She saw a tortured man. Moving on sheer instinct, she grabbed his hand.

Chapter Nine

Why was he standing by his bedroom door afraid to enter the kitchen? Because the woman in there had seen him in too many vulnerable positions, that's why. He felt like a punk.

But, he wasn't. He had been asleep. He couldn't control his dreams, or in this case, his nightmare.

He pressed his ear to the door, listening to Annie puttering around in there. His cast was supposed to come off today. She would be taking him through a new physical therapy regimen today. But, he could do none of that if he didn't open the door.

Saul opened the door and made his way towards her voice. She had the radio on 91.7FM and was singing along to a Christian song. As he listened to her melodious voice, he wondered what she looked like. He imagined her as a blonde, but she was so peppery that he decided she had to be a redhead. A redhead with green eyes.

"What color's your hair?" he bellowed upon his entrance. He heard her squeal of surprise and cracked up.

"Where's your cane?" she asked.

"I didn't need it," Saul said dismissively. "Now answer my question, what color's your hair?"

"It's various shades of brown."

"What about your eyes?"

"Dark brown," she supplied.

So he was wrong on both counts, but he wasn't disappointed. "You sound beautiful," he smiled.

"Thanks," she drawled. "Do you want something to eat?"

He sniffed the air. He smelled eggs and bacon and remembered he hadn't eaten much the night before.

"Yes, I do. You didn't have to cook though. That's what I have Linda, my housekeeper for. She usually comes three times a week to clean and cook my meals." His stomach growled. There was no pretending she didn't hear that.

"I didn't mind, and I don't think your stomach does, either," Annie said, walking away from him.

Saul liked listening to her movements as she retrieved plates and shared their food. His heart tripped. It sounded clichéd but his heart warmed at her presence. "Will you read to me? Psalms 91 again."

"How can I refuse reading you the Bible? Psalms 91 is a powerful piece of scripture because it shows how much God protects us. He was with you during the accident for sure. How many men can say they would be able to walk after a crash like that..."

Saul listened as she rambled on, liking her voice. She had such positivity and promise, which made him feel as if he could do anything.

"I'm going to church this Saturday, and please know, you have an open invite to come with me," Annie stated.

He didn't want to hurt her feelings but it had been ages since he'd stepped foot inside a church. The last time he'd gone had been for his wife's funeral. Nevertheless, he said, "I just might take you up on that."

"I'm more than happy to have you with me. You would love Pastor Noah Charleston. He is a dynamic preacher and expounds on the word so that even a baby can understand. He's on television as well."

Saul smiled. "I've never heard him." If it weren't for Annie's enthusiasm about God, he knew he wouldn't have even entertained the discussion. "Does your pastor do counseling?"

"Yes, he has a degree in mental health counseling. Do you want me to set up an appointment for you?"

"Let me think on it a little," Saul hedged. He'd take things one step at a time.

"Can we talk about last night?" she asked. He could hear uncertainty in her voice and listened keenly. "It sounded like you were having a bad dream. I didn't think to knock. I'm sorry. It won't happen again."

Saul was quick to assure her. "I'm glad you came in and held my hand. It helped. I keep reliving the accident or my fights with my daughter. I can only hope that these will lessen in time."

All of a sudden, he ached for a human connection.

"I know this sounds like an odd request but, can I touch you?" he asked. "I want to know what you look like?"

"Sure. Without your sight, touching is a good way for you to get to know people."

He nodded at her professional tone. His senses heightened as she drew closer to him. When she was in proximity, he lifted his hand to tenderly outline her face. Her skin was smooth and soft. Her nose had a slight tilt and her lips—oh, those lips felt full and luscious.

"You're beautiful." Saul licked his lips, suddenly wanting to place his over hers. Whoa. Where had that thought come from? Caught off guard, Saul moved his hand as if he'd been burnt.

"Afraid I'll bite?" she giggled.

Her laughter tickled his senses, and he cracked up. A kitchen towel made its way to his face. Saul's chest heaved. It'd been awhile since he laughed with such exuberance.

"Well, I must say it feels good to return and hear you laughing. What's so funny?"

Saul tensed. He knew that voice. He swung towards the voice. "Annie, I'd like you to meet—

Annie gave a squeak. "Macy Masters! Macy Masters is   your   girlfriend?"

Chapter Ten

Don't think about her.

Try as she might, it was impossible not to. When Saul mentioned a girlfriend, Annie pictured a beautiful everyday woman—a schoolteacher or a banker, not a supermodel like Macy Masters. Her face was splattered on billboards. She couldn't compete with that.

Not that she was trying to compete, per se. She sniffed. She didn't stand a chance so she might as well get any fancy notions out of her head. Saul viewed her as his therapist and nothing more.

Annie grabbed her coat. She needed to take a drive. She called Sari to see if she was available. Unfortunately, Sari had been called in to work.

She wandered into the kitchen and opened the refrigerator to see if anything inside there enticed her stomach buds.

"In the mood for a snack?"

Annie jumped and slammed the door with a thud. "I didn't see you!"

Macy smiled. She was seated at the breakfast bar crunching on a big bowl of Honey-Nut Cheerios. Annie eyed her with fascination.

"Don't let the tabloids fool you. Many of us do eat and we eat healthy," Macy said.

Annie shook her head. "I wasn't... Well..." She shrugged. "I did believe the stereotype. I would've expected you to be eating wheatgrass or tofu."

Macy threw her head back and chuckled. "I see why Saul likes you."

He liked her? Yeah, but he told his girlfriend, so he didn't *like her* like her. She kept her voice neutral. "I like him too. He's a joy to work with."

Macy arched her brow. "Are we talking about Saul Sweeterman? Because he's a boar when he's sick. He ran us all out of his room. He mentioned you called him on it."

Evidently, Saul told his woman everything. Annie relaxed. "I only told the truth."

"Yes, but you don't get it. Many of us tell him about himself too. He never listens. However, he listens to you."

Annie bit her lip. Macy had a pensive expression on her face. She didn't know what to do, so she re-opened the refrigerator door and pulled out some turkey meat and all the trappings to make a sandwich.

"Ooh, can you make me one?"

Annie's mouth popped open.

"I know what you're thinking," Macy laughed. "Where do I put it? Saul says I eat like a horse."

Annie nodded. "If I ate like that I wouldn't be able to fit through the door."

They heard the click-clack of Saul's cane and turned in his direction. He looked like he'd just awakened from a nap. "I thought I heard noises in here."

"Annie and I were just getting better acquainted," Macy said. "She was talking about how she fears getting fat."

"I don't think she has to worry about that," Saul replied. "She seems very fit to me."

He couldn't see the sharp look Macy threw his way, but Annie could. She busied her hands.

"Do you want a sandwich?"

Saul faced her way. "I told you that you don't have to do any cooking. Macy and I would have gladly ordered carryout."

"It's only a sandwich," she recountered. "Do you want one or not?"

"All right, feisty lady. I'll have two." Saul waved at her.

Macy held a hand towards her. "You, see Annie. That's what I mean."

Saul crooked his head. "Meant about what?"

***

"What did you mean by what you said earlier?" Saul asked Macy that evening. They were lounging in the lanai as Annie had decided to go to the movies. He recognized that was her way of giving he and Macy some privacy.

"You're different with her," Macy said.

Saul wished he could see her face. Something about her tone heightened his senses. "How different?" He reached his hand out to search for hers. He smiled when her fingers grasped his.

"I don't know, exactly. Your face glows."

Saul used his free hand to touch his face in a reflexive action. "I glow."

"Maybe glow isn't the right word. You're happy and you listen to her."

He wasn't sure how to respond to her statement when he couldn't gauge her mood. "So you want me to be angry and nasty?" he chuckled.

He felt her slap his hand. "No, silly. I want you to be nicer to me."

Saul withdrew his hand. "Is this about us not sleeping together? Macy, I'm going through a big ordeal right now and I'm barely finding my way. I thought you understood."

"I know you're going through a difficult time and I can't even begin to imagine what I would do if I…"

Saul gritted his teeth. "Say the words. You don't know what you would do if you were blind. Blind. Blind. I'm blind!"

In a huge swoop, he swung his hand across the table. The lemonade jug and glasses all landed on the tile with a loud crash. Macy inhaled.

"There you go with that awful temper of yours! You need to control yourself. I know you're blind but you don't need your eyes to make love to me. We both have needs and maybe if you got some you wouldn't be so…disagreeable."

"I can't believe you! You've been crowned the most beautiful woman in the world and you're throwing a tantrum because I'm not swooning for you. Forgive me if I've been caught up in the fact that I can't see!"

Her heels protested as she dragged the chair across the tile. Her heels hit the floor with a vengeance. Where was she going? Within seconds, Saul heard Macy's muttering and heard the vigorous sweeping of a broom.

"Move your feet!" she commanded.

Saul complied. He released a long breath. "Macy, I'm sorry." He heard a hiccup and knew she was crying. "Darling, please don't cry."

"You like her. Admit it. That's why you won't touch me. You have her in your bedroom and we're sleeping in separate bedrooms."

Saul wasn't about to admit to something he wasn't sure about. "You never liked my bedroom, remember? You said the color scheme was depressing which is why you decorated your bedroom down the hall."

"Yes, but…"

"But, what? You told me you liked Annie. You said she was good for me."

"But that was before I saw you with her."

Saul lifted his hands to the heavens. "I'll never understand how the female mind works. Macy, you've never been the jealous type. You've never questioned or wondered about my loyalty before."

"She's beautiful," Macy supplied.

He'd wondered about that but he knew better than to continue that conversation thread. Instead he asked, "What makes Annie different from the countless women you've seen me with at the dealership?

"I don't know. Why don't you tell me? What makes Annie different from all the other women at the dealership?"

Chapter Eleven

"I'm sure your girlfriend would've been happy to take you," Annie declared.

"You're right. She would have but Macy is jet-lagged. I couldn't ask her to drive me down here. Besides, she has another job in Japan. This is a brief layover. She'll be gone again in a day of two. He wasn't about to admit that he and Macy had gotten into a fight because of her.

Truthfully, Saul hated that Annie had to be his guide. He wasn't use to depending on anyone and he wanted to drive himself into town and handle his business. "I'll be back in a minute." He made it out of the car but cringed when Annie had to get out to help into the front door.

"Saul!" Greg greeted him.

Saul gripped Greg's arm. "I came to see how things are going," he joked.

"I've got him," Greg said. Saul knew he was talking to Annie.

"I'll be in the car," she said.

Within thirty minutes, he was in her car and they were back on the road.

"How's everything?" she asked.

"Greg has everything under control and he went over my earnings assuring me all is well," Saul replied.

"It must feel good to have those around you whom you can trust."

"Yes, it does. He was with me from day one. I trust him with everything. He's Cassandra's godfather. Speaking of which, he urged me to pay her a visit. Would you mind if we went by her house?"

"No, what's the address?"

Saul recited the address that Greg had provided. He didn't want to tell Annie that he'd never set foot in his daughter's home—didn't even know where she lived. Her house was twenty minutes away from his dealership in the next town.

"Is she expecting you?"

He knew the question she was really asking, and answered, "No, but I'm going anyway. If I wait on Cassandra to respond to me, I might enter another lifetime. Greg advised me to just show up."

"I agree with him," Annie said. "My family lives in Jacksonville, and believe me, if I were freezing my parents out, they'd be at my door."

A thought occurred to him as she mentioned her parents. "How do your parents feel about you living with me?"

He heard her hesitate before she said in a low voice,

"I didn't tell them."

"Say what?" Saul wished he could see her face. He used her voice as cues to determine how she was feeling but there was nothing like being able to look a person in their face.

"I don't know why I didn't tell them," she confessed. "I've also limited my conversation with them to about five minutes, or else I'll be spilling the proverbial beans."

"But this is a job," he retorted. "You're a professional. I can't see why you wouldn't inform them."

"I can," she said. "My mother would insist on seeing a picture of you and if she did—

Her voice trailed off as she put the car in park. They must have arrived at their destination. Saul sat forward in his seat and reached for her hand. "If she did, what?" he wanted to know. He discerned she really didn't want to answer, but waited her out. He wasn't moving until she answered.

"Well, let's just say that she would think my moving in with you had nothing to do with a job, and she would be right."

He smiled, loving the ego boost from her bold words. Annie, however, was done talking and exited the vehicle. He jumped from the loud slam of her door and within seconds, she opened his side and proclaimed, "We're here!"

Saul gripped her hand. His throat felt dry, his palms sweaty and his heart was beating so loud that he was convinced all of Northport would hear it.

"Have you changed your mind?"

He heard the sympathy in her tone and resented it. "No, and for the record, I don't need coddling. I can get there on my own two feet."

She sucked her teeth, and said, "Suit yourself." He heard her flip-flops as she left him to fend for himself. The thing was he couldn't see where he was going. He reached behind him for the cane, but paused.

Saul exhaled and his shoulders slumped. Why had he done that? He had no reason for attacking the one person who was helping him and putting up with his nasty attitude. "Annie, I'm sorry," he said. "I shouldn't have snapped off at you like I did. You've been in my corner and all I've done is push you away. It's hard for me to admit, but I need you."

"Okay, I forgive you." Her cheerful tone made him wonder at her sanity. Was she really over it, or was she going to make him pay?

"You accept my apology?" he creased his eyebrows, not understanding.

"Yes, I do. What did you expect me to do? Rant and rave and carry on? You said you're sorry and I accept it."

Saul shook his head. "Annie Hays, I think it's safe to say I've never met anyone like you."

She took his hands in one of her hands and placed her other hand on top of his head so he wouldn't hit it as he got out of the car. Then she guided him to the front door.

"Your leg is coming along nicely," she remarked. "I think Dr. Pryor will recommend more strenuous activities when we go in to see him next week."

Saul harrumphed but said nothing. He asked Annie to ring the doorbell and attempted to compose himself as he heard a little voice yell, "Mommy! Mommy! Someone's at the door!"

"Go in your room!" he heard his daughter say. Saul steeled himself. He reached his hand over to Annie's searching until she clasped her hand in his. He sighed with relief. Now, he was ready.

The door swung open and he heard a high-pitched, "Dad? What're you doing here? Where's Macy? And, why are you here with *her?*"

Saul was a bit put off by her tone. He played the father card. He turned his head, and prayed he was looking her in the eyes. "Cassandra, you've ignored my calls and now it sounds like you're being rude to my guest. If you must know, Macy is at home resting. She has a big job coming up." He wasn't about to elaborate any further. He continued, "Now, are you going to let us in? Or, are you going to broadcast our business for the neighbors to hear?"

Chapter Twelve

Count to ten.

She bit the inside of her cheeks following the Holy Ghost directions. If it weren't for Him, she'd wrap that corn silk hair around her hands at that "And, with her?" comment.

Ten—nine –eight—*Let it go, Annie, let it go.*

Naw, but what did she mean by *her?*

The old Annie would've turned on her heels and returned to her car at Saul's daughter's belligerent tone. She knew that look and what it meant. Cassandra wanted to know why her father was at her home with a black woman. She'd seen that sneer enough times to know.

Instead, she held herself upright, led Saul into the home and settled him onto the couch. Once she was sure he was situated, Annie announced, "I'll be back. I'm going to T. J. Maxx."

Cassandra rushed over and touched Annie on the arm. "May I speak with you a minute?" The young woman gestured towards the kitchen. It took Holy

Ghost power for her not to shrug the other woman off, but she followed.

"I'm sorry for how I sounded. It's just that I would've never expected my father to show up here with a black woman," the young woman whispered. Her friendly eyes tempered the implication behind her words.

Annie arched her eyebrow. "Yes, I'm black. So what?" she snipped. Really, in this day and age, she was sick of racism masked under polite southern gentility. Never mind that Port Charlotte had plenty of interracial couples, the racist attitudes were just as prevalent.

Cassandra took a small step back at her tone. Annie resisted the urge to go off on her. She bit her lip determined not to live up to the stereotype of the angry, black woman. She also didn't want to make Cassandra nervous.

"Cassie, are you going to make me sit here all day? Because I'm not leaving until we talk!" Saul called out.

"I'm getting you lemonade and talking with Annie for a minute. I'm coming," Cassandra yelled back.

The younger woman twisted her fingers. "I'm saying this all wrong," she explained. In a whisper she continued, "My father has never dated outside his race. In fact, he's quite against it. Did he tell you that he and I haven't spoken in four years because I married a black man?"

Her mouth popped open. "We're not dating, or did you forget about Macy?" her brain just caught up with Cassandra's revelation. Had she heard right? "Did you say he didn't speak to you because you married a black man?"

"Yes, and my husband died without my father's blessing. He's never even seen or spoken to his granddaughter because of his refusal to accept what he calls a mixed breed."

Annie held her hands up. She couldn't comprehend what she was hearing. She shook her head finding it hard to reconcile the monster that Cassandra painted with the man she was coming to know and even falling—no. He had a girlfriend. She wouldn't entertain that thought. "I need some air. I'll be back. No, wait, can you take him home for me?"

Her blue eyes depicted understanding. "He doesn't know, does he?"

"Mommy, can I come out, now?"

Annie's eyes zoomed in on the most beautiful child she'd ever seen.

"Emily, meet Miss Annie," Cassandra said, bending towards her daughter. Emily hid behind her mother's skirt and peeked at Annie. "It's okay, honey. Can you shake Miss Annie's hand and say hello?"

"Hi, Miss Annie. I'm Emily and I'm three years old." The little girl held up three stubby fingers and Annie's heart melted. She was so precious, how could Saul deny his own flesh and blood?

She couldn't help the tears that sprung to her eyes. She stooped, until she was on Emily's level. "Hi, Emily. It's such a pleasure to meet you."

Emily smiled, before looking up at her mother. "Can I go watch television?"

"Yes, honey."

Emily skipped off towards the living area, where she would meet her grandfather for the first time. A grandfather who wouldn't be able to see her. It was all too much for Annie to handle. She put a fist in her mouth, trying to keep her emotions in check.

"I—I need to think. Go talk to him." Annie spun on her heels and departed from the house. She ran from the ugly stench of prejudice, which had reared its head, attacking her growing love like a parasite.

As she raced out the driveway, she called herself all kinds of idiot. Here she was pining after someone who didn't know the real her? She looked in the rearview mirror seeing her natural curls, her brown eyes, her coffee-colored skin. If she were fat, she could lose weight. If she had bad skin, she could treat it. If she had crooked teeth, she could get braces. But, there was nothing she could do about this. She couldn't—and didn't want to—change the color of her skin.

Overcome, she pulled into a parking space outside the shopping center. She choked back the floodgate of tears. The doctors had said that Saul could regain his vision without warning. How would he react if he saw her in his kitchen—in his home? Would his face transform into one of disgust?

Annie couldn't take that chance. She wasn't about to stick around and watch his face curl with scorn. She loved every inch of her black skin. She wasn't going to let any man make her feel less than desirable. Not now. Not ever.

Chapter Thirteen

"I was an idiot," he said.

Seated next to his daughter, Saul wished he could see her face. The two hours he'd been there had sped by. Cassandra had told him that Annie had gone shopping and she'd volunteered to drive him home. He welcomed this time with his daughter, determined to make up for lost time.

"Yes, you were," his daughter agreed. "How could you have thrown our relationship away like I meant nothing to you? How could you ask me to choose between you and my husband? Then you wonder why I didn't answer the phone."

He heard the tears in her voice and pictured her lips quivering like she always did when she was about to cry but didn't want to. "It was never about you, Cassandra. It was the way I was raised. From a child, I can remember the words I heard, and the things my parents said. I didn't think to question it. I wish I had loved you enough to give Kellan a chance."

"You would've loved him, Dad," Cassandra gushed. From her tone Saul realized she was eager to talk about her husband. He heard her wistful tone and knew she was grieving. He knew about that kind of grief. "Kellan reminded me so much of you. If you'd just taken a chance to know him, you would've liked him."

Saul felt a little discomfort at being compared to her husband. He gulped, not sure of what to say. He knew she expected a response. "I'm sorry I won't get the opportunity to prove you right. No matter what I said, I didn't wish him dead. Cassandra, I hope you know that," he beseeched her, with deep regret. "My behavior might have been monstrous, but I would never wish your husband any harm." He was surprised to find how much he meant those words.

"When Kellan and I left that morning, I had no idea it would be my last time seeing his handsome face. He was a wonderful husband and a caring, considerate father."

Saul paused. He'd felt that way about Nora. He swallowed. "I'm glad you have good things to say about your husband. I'm sorry Emily will grow up without a father."

"Do you mean that, Dad. Or, are you saying what you think I want to hear?"
"When have you known me not to speak my mind? I know I didn't approve of the marriage, but I didn't want him dead."

He heard a great sigh. Then her arms surrounded his in a hug. "I shouldn't have blamed you for his death. I know you tried to save us."

He choked up. "I did, honey. I tried to save *all* of you. You must believe that I wouldn't want your daughter to grow up without a father in her life. That's the last thing I would wish for anyone. I know what it's like to lose a spouse so suddenly. It's a shock to your system and you don't know how you'll ever recover. When I lost your mother, I felt that pain for years. I was in a dark place for quite some time. If it weren't for you..."

He felt Cassandra's body heave with tears. "I miss Kellan so much. I put up a good front for Emily but every night I cry myself to sleep."

As she cried, her heartache ripped him to the core. He comforted her, glad that Emily was down for a nap and wouldn't witness her mother's breakdown.

"It's okay to cry, honey. Cry for as long as you have to," he soothed. "It may be too late, but I will be here for you and Emily. I want to know her. I know I don't deserve it but please give me that chance."

"I wish you could actually see her. She has your nose and sometimes your expressions. I swear it's like I see you looking at me."

Saul touched her hair to make contact. "I can just imagine that. I know I'm blind, but I can see her, Cassie. I can hear her laughter. I can feel her joy."

Cassandra moved out of his arms. He heard her blowing her nose and reached over to give her another hug. He felt her tense up but was glad she didn't pull away.

"I can see that you're changing and trying." His daughter addressed him. "I would like us to continue to work on mending our relationship. I know I didn't answer your calls or message and I'm sorry for that. I've been seeing a therapist and funny enough, she'd recommended I reach out to you."

He felt and heard movements. Cassandra had gotten up to go somewhere.

Saul turned his head towards her when he heard her address him from the far corner of the room. "What's going on with Annie?"

"Nothing's going on with Annie. She's my therapist. Why does everyone think that?" he wondered aloud. Was he giving off some vibe around her?

Like Macy, Cassandra seemed fixated on Annie. "If she's just your therapist, then why were you holding hands when I opened the door?"

His smile crumbled. "I was?" He racked his brain. He vaguely remembered reaching for Annie's hand.

"Yes, you were. Don't pretend like you don't remember. You like her, don't you?" Cassandra asked.

Saul grinned. He knew he sounded like a schoolboy. "Yes, I do. In fact, if I weren't afraid of busting my butt, I would pull a Tom Cruise and hop on your couch like a raving maniac. That's how good I'm feeling."

"What if she... wasn't what you... expect, physically, I mean?"

He didn't miss her hesitation. Was there something about Annie that he didn't know? "Is she ugly?" He didn't care if he sounded flaky. He had a feeling his daughter was holding something from him. "No don't tell me, she's has a hideous birthmark?"

"Would it matter?"

Her curiosity was evident in her high-pitched

squeal. He gave her question serious thought. Surprised, he answered, "No, I don't think so. To me, she's beautiful. She's positive, she's bubbly, and she's forgiving. She has a hot temper to match, too." Annie was no pushover and he loved that.

"I know you're adamant that she's your therapist, but if I didn't know better, I would think you're in love."

Saul heard her teasing tone and opened his mouth to respond, but couldn't find the words. Was he in love? The mere idea was ridiculous. It was too soon. He had a girlfriend—one who thought he liked Annie. "Well you do know better. What would I want with Annie when I have Macy by my side?"

He'd diverted the conversation but inside his heart was somersaulting. He couldn't be falling in love with someone he barely knew. If he were going to fall in love then Macy would be the prime candidate. Not Annie. Then why was she filling his thoughts?

All he knew was that he'd been away from Annie long enough. He was ready to go home—to her.

Chapter Fourteen

"Annie left." Those were Macy's words when he entered his home. She must have been waiting for him by the front door to deliver the news.

"What do you mean she left?" Saul asked.

"I don't know why she left."

Saul clenched a fist. "What did you say to her?" he grounded out. "I hope you didn't mention our ridiculous conversation the other day."

He dug into his pockets to get his phone. He was going to call her and demand an explanation.

He felt Macy's breath in his face. "You're blaming me? I don't believe you! It's not my fault she left. I didn't say anything to your precious Annie."

Saul's head snapped back. "She's not my precious Annie. She's my therapist."

"If she's just a therapist, then why does it matter?" Macy grabbed his face with both her hands. "I asked her several times not to go but she was moving like a whirlwind. Before she left, she told me she had arranged for another therapist to come."

He lowered his head and Macy released her hands. For some reason Annie had left him high and dry. Who does that? And, wasn't she supposed to be a Christian?

"I'm leaving tomorrow," Macy said, interrupting his thoughts.

Saul nodded.

"I'm not coming back," she announced.

"What?" Saul swiped the air trying to find her. She moved into his space. "Why are you leaving?"

"I'm done," Macy stated. He heard her voice catch. "I'm not going to stick around pining for someone who doesn't want me. I have thousands of men who want me and I'm tired of the scraps of affection you throw my way. I'm a supermodel. I refuse to play second fiddle to a therapist."

Saul stood where he was as he contemplated her words. He knew this was the moment for him to beg her stay. Perhaps propose or something. Macy was right. He wasn't being fair to her. He couldn't utter the words she needed to hear.

Saul reached under her head to pull her face close to his. His lips found hers with alarming accuracy. He kissed her long and hard before pulling away. "Goodbye, Macy."

She sniffed. "I'll wait until the new person comes and then I'll be gone. It's been good. I'll leave my key in the palm before I leave."

***

"Look, sir. It's as I said. Ms. Hays had an emergency and had to leave this position. I'm her replacement. I'm also a certified orientation and mobility specialist."

Saul snarled. This was the third time he'd asked and gotten this response. In a fit of rage, he took his cane and hurled it. By the crash, he guessed it had broken a window. He didn't really care. He'd spent the night before tossing and turning upset that Annie was gone.

Large hands gripped his shoulders. "Saul, I'm going to have to ask you to calm down."

Saul exhaled. He knew the man before him had to be well over six feet because he seemed like the incredible hulk.

"You don't understand. I need Annie." He knew he sounded whiny, but he didn't give two cents how the other man might perceive him.

"Annie is unavailable."

Corey sounded like he was talking through gritted teeth. Saul knew he wasn't going to get any information from him. He needed to remain calm and think. "Corey, if it's not too much trouble, would you please give me my cell phone."

"You mean the one that you tossed across the room earlier?"

How he hated that ingratiating voice near his ear! He gritted his teeth and clenched his fists, resisting the urge to knock Corey senseless—well try to. "Yes, the same one."

Corey released him and he heard his large footfall as the other man retrieved his cell phone. Saul was glad that he'd bought the Otter Box or he would be purchasing yet another phone.

"Hold out your hand," Corey said. This time he sounded neutral and Saul was glad for that. He had to trust that whomever Annie had sent in as her replacement was reliable. How he hated being without his sight.

"Do you need me to dial the number?"

"No, I don't need you to dial the number," Saul replied nastily. "I lost my sight, not my brain. I'm capable of operating a cell phone."

"Just asking." Corey placed the phone in his hands.

Saul complied and curled his fingers around his phone. He played nice until he was settled into his bedroom upstairs. There was no way he was letting Corey take his room. He'd have the younger man move his things upstairs. Saul was now competent at climbing stairs. He counted steps and his cane helped.

He called Cassandra to check up on her and to speak with Emily. He kept his conversation lighthearted, not wanting his daughter to discern that while he was exchanging pleasantries, his heart was tearing against his flesh. He had too much pride to tell her about Annie's departure.

He settled against his pillows and made another call. This time he heard the swirl before a computer-operated voice informed him, "The number you were trying to reach has calling restrictions which has prevented the completion of your call."

"Huh?" confused, he tried again.

The same message.

"No, this can't be right," he said, hitting the end button. He dialed her number again.

He almost convulsed when he heard, "The number you've—"

Annie had blocked his calls!

"Ugh!" Saul threw his phone. He heard a satisfied thud. It dropped to the floor. Sort of how she'd dropped him.

Chapter Fifteen

"You've made a big mistake," Sari declared, rubbing her nose. You shouldn't have left like that. You owed it to yourself and Saul. You don't know how he would've reacted."

The two friends had met up by Fisherman's village and taken an impromptu sail across the Peace River. The water rocked beneath them as they sat across from each other and settled in to their discussion.

"He would've paid me and kicked me to the curb, disguised under the politeness of southern gentility, of course," she snorted. Annie wiped her face with tissues she'd stuffed in her purse. Her face was red and puffy from crying but she was past the point of caring. She'd been crying at the apartment for hours before Sari called and suggested they get together to discuss her wedding plans. Now here she sat on the water, crying for a man who would think she was way too many shades darker than his preference.

"There you go jumping to conclusions. You don't know what he would've done if you'd confronted him head on. Instead, you shirked away like someone who's ashamed of her heritage and her people."

Annie's temper flared. "I'm not ashamed of myself or my race, thank you very much and let's not forget the man has a supermodel for a girlfriend. I'm sure Saul Sweeterman will be just fine."

Sari grinned. "There's my friend. The one I'm used to seeing." The wind picked up and Sari's hair went all helter skelter.

Annie groped for the extra ponytail holder she kept in her purse and handed it to her friend. "Normally, I would have been up in his face after hearing that story from his daughter. I mean when Cassandra told me that her dad refused to see her and even her baby—his own flesh and blood, I said to myself, what would he do to me? I wanted to storm into that house and show him the size of my angry black woman hat, but then…" she gulped. "My heart. My heart's involved. I just didn't have the guts to…" She put her head into her hands. "I hate that I have feelings for him because it affected my standing up for who I am."

Sari moved to slide next to her and huddled her close. "You can't help who you have feelings for, Annie."

Annie nodded, "Yes—yes, you can. You have a choice about who you love."

"No you don't," Sari disagreed. "You don't decide who makes you heart curl like an armadillo. The only decision you make is a commitment to that love. God loves us. We didn't ask for it. We can't change it. But, we can decide whether or not to accept His love."

"Right now, if I could stop my heart from feeling what it's feeling I would." Sari's words came back to her. She digressed, "Only someone in Florida would use an armadillo as a metaphor."

Sari cracked up. "Whatever. I was trying to be poetic but you get the point. Annie, what if he's the one God has for you?"

"Then God has a cruel sense of humor. I can't see God putting me together with a bigot."

"True. But I can see God using you to teach Saul a lesson in love. God loved Saul enough to spare his life from an accident that killed two other people—his son-in-law and the truck driver. From the police report, we know that Saul had put himself in harm's way. God shielded him for a reason—two actually.

God wants Saul for a purpose and you're the person He's going to use to lead him to it. Two, God knows you needed a man. Girl, all you do is work. Is there any surprise that the good Lord had to deposit the man right under your nose for you to notice him?"

Annie slapped her friend's arm unable to stifle her laugh. "You're wrong for that and I'm sure Macy would not agree. I don't have time for a social life. I'm working towards buying my home."

"Well, if you hadn't run off, you wouldn't need to buy a home or anything else," Sari said.

Annie shook her head. "You seem to forget his girlfriend. I keep having to mention her."

"I haven't forgotten her," her friend stated. "But you should know that unless there's a ring, it don't mean a thing."

"How could I forget?" Annie thought she had been Cornell Adam's true love but a week after she'd broken things off with him; he placed a huge rock on another woman's finger.

A thought occurred to her. "Do you think Cassandra will tell him?" Annie was hopeful. If his daughter told him then she wouldn't have that task.

"Who knows? Although I think he and Cassandra have way too much to talk about besides you. That's what I think."

Annie shook her head. She shifted the subject. "Will you pray with me?"

Sari's demeanor changed. She took Annie's hands in hers and bowed her head. "Lord, speak to both Annie and Saul. I know You've brought them together. Reveal Your divine purpose and plan for them. Lord, make the path clear. Lead and guide them into Your perfect will. I pray this prayer, in Jesus' name. Amen."

Annie smiled, comforted. Prayer had a way of doing that for her.

***

If he were a praying man, he'd be on his knees now. It had been one month since Annie's departure and though he still wore the cast, his leg was healing nicely. During a consult, Dr. Pryor had told him that he might have a slight limp. However, Saul wasn't worried. He'd been fit before the accident so that worked in his favor with his recovery.

He didn't want to admit it, but Corey was an excellent therapist. He just wasn't Annie.

Speaking of Annie. She filled his thoughts. Whenever he went in for rehab, Saul hoped to hear her voice but she'd made herself scarce. Somehow, he knew that had been on purpose, and it hurt.

Saul heard the doorbell and made his way towards the door. He heard Emily's voice outside calling, "Grandpa! Grandpa!"

With a huge smile, he opened the door to welcome his daughter and granddaughter inside. "What a great surprise. I wasn't expecting you to drop by."

"We were in the neighborhood," Cassandra said.

"Oh, you answered the door." Corey asked as he came up behind him. He heard Corey's soft, "Hi, Cassandra. You're looking lovely as usual."

Saul rolled his eyes, not caring if the younger man saw his actions. Corey was tough as nails until his daughter was present. Whenever she visited, he morphed into some soppy idiot. Saul grimaced. He hoped he didn't sound like that with Annie.

"Thanks, Corey. How's my dad progressing?"

"As you can see everything's improving, except his surly attitude."

Both of them laughed. Saul waved him off. "Aren't you late for your workout?"

"Actually, I was thinking of using your pool. Emily, do you want to go swimming?"

"Yippee!!!" Emily grabbed Corey's hand. Within minutes, Saul heard peals of laughter coming from behind them.

Cassandra kept her end of the conversation professional. Saul knew it was because she'd just buried her husband whom she loved deeply. Since Kellan's death, Cassandra had focused on Emily and now him. Counseling was her grief solution. She didn't have any desire for anyone else. Saul had been the opposite when Nora passed. He worked out his pain in the arms of nameless women before dating Macy and now, even that affair had ended.

Unaware of his thoughts, Cassandra said, "He's so thoughtful. I think he took her so we could talk without her present."

"Corey's all right. He's a good swimmer and lifeguard. I've done some of my therapy sessions in the water. That man has so many certifications..." The conversation stilled. He sensed Cassie's quietness. "What's on your mind?"

"I'm concerned about you. Why didn't you tell me that you and Macy had broken up? I only know because Uncle Greg told me you turned down his offer to call some of your *friends* to cheer you up."

He read between the lines. "I'm not interested in getting with any friends, as you so delicately phrased it. I have every intention of living a full life but I'm not going to settle. I tried with Macy and it didn't work. I think its time I find someone to grow old with. Someone who wants something more meaningful than shopping sprees and high heels."

"So what you're really saying is, you want Annie?"

He shrugged. "I think she's blocked my number."

"Then you need to go to her."

"I don't know where she lives."

"But you know where she works," Cassie said.

"Yes, but she's been avoiding me."

"There's one place she can't avoid you," she teased. "You need to face her on neutral territory—church."

Why hadn't he thought of that? Saul straightened. "Cassie, how'd you and Emily like to come with me to church?"

"What time will you be ready?"

Chapter Sixteen

CHECK OUT THE THIRD ROW ON YOUR RIGHT.

Annie read the text message from Sari. From the second row of the choir section, she scanned the crowd. Sari's text could be anything from a fine man to a ridiculous hat. She didn't know what to expect but she knew it was bound to be entertaining.

Her eyes bulged. What was Saul doing here? Yes, she'd invited him, but that was a month ago and she didn't think he would still come. His family sat next to him. Macy wasn't there. Annie admitted to herself that she didn't mind that at all.

She squinted to roam Saul's frame. His dark blue suit and baby blue shirt made his eyes popped. She resisted the urge to fan herself. The only comfort was that he couldn't see her. She drunk in the sight of him and admitted how much she missed him and how glad she was that he was here.

She sent Sari a furtive reply: IS GOD TRYING TO TELL ME SOMETHING?

HE AIN'T TRYIN, HE IS shot back at her.

An older sister nudged her in the arm and raised her eyebrows. "Sorry," Annie whispered, contrite. She knew better than to be texting in church. She put the device away. Her eyes wandered at will until they rested on Saul. Wistful, she smiled at his presence, until she locked eyes with Cassandra. When the younger woman gave her a small wave, she nodded but turned her attention to the message.

Pastor Noah Charleston took the pulpit. "Today, I feel led to talk about Esther. Now God isn't mentioned in the book, but her life depicted an example of Christ that is relevant for us today. Esther was chosen, placed by God, into the king's house because she had a greater purpose. She was meant to save His people."

Annie felt awareness creep up her spine. She felt as if the message was meant for her. It was like God was showing her that she was an Esther placed into Saul's home—a home without God. She shrugged. Maybe she was reading too much into the sermon.

The pastor continued. "Now Esther knew her purpose but her task would require that she enter the king's chamber without permission. To enter without being summoned meant certain death, unless the king raised the scepter offering a pardon—a pardon that wasn't guaranteed. She called a three-day fast before she put her life on the line." He was warming up. "But, it wasn't about her life, it was about the life of God's people. In the end, God cares about a soul. I'm convinced that even if it were to save one soul, He still would've left His throne in heaven for one person. Friends, Jesus left heaven for you. He is standing in the gap, as Esther stood in the gap."

She relaxed. Maybe it was a stretch of her imagination that this was for her.

"How many of us can say we've been an 'Esther' for someone. How many of us have called a fast for someone? How many of us can say we have stood in the gap for another soul?"

Annie covered her mouth with her hand. She couldn't say that she had stood in the gap for Saul and she should have. She bent her head and uttered a prayer to God. Pastor Charleston made an altar call. She craned her neck to see if Saul was coming forward. He remained in his row, but bowed his head in supplication. Cassandra came forward with little Emily clutching her hand.

What about you?

Annie jumped to her feet in obeisance to the voice of God. She approached the altar and raised her hands in prayer. As the service concluded, she made her way through the congregation to greet Cassandra.

"I enjoyed the service so much, I'll definitely come again." Her smile was bright and her eyes shone. "I love the way he explained the word so that I could understand." Annie agreed. "This is how he is every week. Do you want me to introduce you to him?" The longer she could avoid facing Saul the better. She had no idea what she was going to say to him.

Cassandra shook her head. "Next week. I've got to get back to my dad. He looks lost over there."

"Not too lost," Annie returned. The women were flocking to him like vultures. The church sisters—black and white—were surrounding him, circling him. You would think they had never seen a handsome man before. Her stomach clenched. She didn't like the attention he was receiving. From where she stood, she heard his bellow of laughter and cut her eyes.

She caught Cassandra's knowing look but said nothing. Even though jealousy burned a hole in her insides, she would never admit how affected she was.

"Won't you come over later? I'm sure he'd love to see you."

"That's the problem. I don't think he'd love to see me."

Cassandra's face mirrored regret. "I wish I'd never said anything. I've never seen my dad so…" Annie looked at Cassandra but she shook her head as if to say, she didn't have the words.

Was he as miserable as she was? If so, that was a small measure of comfort, because she'd been miserable this past month. So miserable that she passed on going to see her family for Independence Day. Annie wasn't ready to face her parents' curiosity and questions.

With her heart in her throat, she went over to Saul. He turned in her direction. If she didn't know better, she'd think he was looking her right in the eyes. She squirmed.

"Dad, look who came over to say hello."

"How could you leave like that?" he asked, heedless to the onlookers. Saul's voice rose, "I called and called. You blocked my number."

Annie gave Cassandra a wide-eyed glare. She couldn't believe he'd put her on blast like that. "Hello to you too, Saul. How have you been? I'm well." She grabbed his arm and forced him to walk with her. Under her breath, she dictated, "Thanks for embarrassing me."

He lacked the decency to apologize. Instead, he griped, "I don't care how you feel. You didn't care about my feelings when you disappeared. You left me. Why?"

She drew in a deep breath and held onto her control until they stepped outside the sanctuary. The sun's glare caught her off guard and she whipped out her sunglasses to shield her eyes from the sun. "You should put on your shades. You still need protection from the sun's harsh rays," she grumbled. She was still put out with him.

He reached into his shirt pocket, grabbed his frames and put them on.

"I had a good reason for leaving." Annie picked up the conversation where they left off.

She saw his eyebrows shoot up and he crossed his arms. "I'm waiting."

His tone got on her last nerve. "It's nothing that I want to get into," Annie said. "How's Corey working out?"

Thankfully, he followed her conversation shift. She wasn't about to address the race issue here in public. She didn't want to touch it at all. How could he be so… backwards?

"He's quite good, although he's the size of a gorilla. As you can see, I'm progressing well. My heart is another matter." He didn't bother to disguise the hurt he was feeling.

He reached out to find her face. He ran his hand across her cheek. She couldn't control the goose bumps.

"You feel it, too. Don't you?" he asked removing his hand.

She shook her head. "I don't know what you're talking about?"

He arched an eyebrow. "The attraction between us. Don't even bother denying it." He reached out searching the air for her hand.

Annie inhaled, before putting her hand in his. His thumb circled her wrist and she shivered.

Her heart skipped a beat. "What about Macy?" She had to ask.

"She's gone."

She took a huge gulp. Gone sounded permanent. Hope sprung. Annie decided to be upfront with her feelings. She rushed out, "Saul, it was hard for me to go without saying goodbye. If it were possible, I think I would've died this past month from heartache."

He took a step towards her. "Then come back. We need to talk. I deserve an explanation. I—I—"

Annie cut him off, afraid of what he might say. "I'll come by later next week. I promise."

"Make that first thing in the morning," he commanded.

Cassandra and Emily spotted them and made their way over to join them. Annie felt relieved at their presence. She excused herself under the premise that Sari was her ride. As she walked away, all Annie could see was Saul's tortured face. With each step, she tried to remember that she was falling for a man who would most likely revolt at the sight of her.

She approached Sari's neon green Toyota Camry on leaden feet.

"I was half-expecting to hear that you were leaving with them," Sari commented.

"I'm going to meet up with him tomorrow. I've no idea what I'm going to say."

"How about the truth?" Sari urged. "Like I suggested when you came home and went straight for the double fudge ice cream."

"I was a mess," Annie said, recalling the day she left Saul's house. After she snatched her belongings from Saul's house, she'd driven home on autopilot. She wasn't even sure if she observed the basic traffic rules. All she knew was, she entered her home curled up under her covers and binged on ice cream. It was her way of licking her wounds.

No matter how far blacks had come as a race, for Annie, it ached to know that there were some who would always see her race as inferior. She could recall countless times a cashier would barely want to touch her hand to give her a receipt—looking down his or her nose at her as if she were trash. Humph, she had career. Sometimes she copped an attitude, but most of the time, she just let it slide. Ignorant people were everywhere.

When she met Saul she hadn't gotten that vibe. He

was angry, yes. Ornery, yes. But, not once did she think he could be prejudiced. He had several pictures displayed in his home with a tall black man whom he said was his best friend. She supposed friendship was all right—nothing else. No mixing of the races. She shook her head. How could he turn his back on his daughter for years? And, Emily? She was his grandchild. Who did that?

"I'm afraid to confront him because I'm afraid of what he'll say," Annie confessed. She felt like her heart was breaking. How had she done this? How had she put her heart out there again?

Sari removed one hand from the steering wheel to squeeze her hand. "I hate to see you like this, but you can't outrun your feelings. I tried. When my son died, I thought I would die. I thought the best thing to do was to carry on and wipe out all signs of his existence from my life. Remember, I didn't even mention his name for almost a year, but I was wrong. Instead, I had to confront the pain and celebrate Lucas's life by talking about him."

Sari turned into their complex and pulled into one of the designated parking spots. Annie took her hand to keep her from exiting the car. "That was such a terrible time, Sari. What I'm feeling is insignificant foolishness compared to your reality. You lost a child. I only lost the man I love."

"Stop. Wait. Did you say *love?*"

Annie bent her head. "Yes, love. There's no use denying it. It sounds like a cliché but I must have fallen for him the moment I met him." She turned towards her friend, and entreated, "What am I going to do?"

"You're going to fight. If you love him, you have to tell him the truth. Tell him and put yourself out there."

"And face rejection?" She shook her head. "There's no way I'm going to put myself out there like that. "

"If you don't put yourself out there, you'll regret it. You'll end up a spinster with those oversized rollers in your hair, who is always scratching her butt."

Annie laughed at Sari's Carol Burnett analogy. "Be nice."

Sari got serious. "God has that man alive for a reason and I can't help but feel you're that reason."

Annie touched her chin. "Granted, God could be calling him but that doesn't mean he's for me. I know a lot of Christians who love God but still hold on to their prejudices."

"Girl, do I need to remind you of Kirk Franklin's song? It doesn't matter what color you are, as long your blood runs red. When it comes to interracial dating, people are always going to have a problem with it. Some people will give you bad looks and others will resent you, but if you crack under the pressure then it wasn't love. Love bears all things, endures all things…" she trailed off and waited for Annie to complete the verse.

"Believes all things," Annie whispered. "In my head, I know you're right. I've got to believe in God's power. I'll put my trust in Him. What God has for me is for me and if Saul's the one, then no one—not even me can mess with that."

"Amen! Sometimes, you've got to let go and let God," Sari preached. "Start praying and share God with him. Concentrate on helping him develop a relationship with God. You want a man who is hearing and listening to God, believe me. You do that and let God do the rest. It'll all work out."

Annie took Sari's words to heart. She closeted herself into her room and devoted herself in a time of prayer. At one point, she dropped to her knees. "Lord, here I am standing in the gap for Saul. He's stubborn and hardheaded but he needs You. I'm thankful that You've brought him into my life and I know now that it was for this purpose. Help me be a light to him. Help me be an example and lead him to You. Lord, I love him, but I know nobody can love him like You can. So take his heart and shape it and make him into a vessel to be used by You. I ask all this through the name of Jesus Christ, my Lord and Savior. Amen."

When she stood, she smiled.

Chapter Seventeen

"Annie's coming by tomorrow. So this might mean, I'll be leaving you soon," Corey informed him Wednesday morning of the following week.

He hadn't even gotten the words out fully before Saul walked towards the front door with sure steps. Making his way to the front door, Saul swung it open and said, "It's been a pleasure working with you."

"You're just going to dismiss me like that?"

Saul joked, "Yes. I'm not even going to pretend I'm not happy Annie's coming back."

"You might as well shut the door and curb your enthusiasm because I'm not going to leave you here on your own."

Saul closed the door. "I know. I couldn't resist."

To his chagrin, Corey laughed. "I've never seen a man so whipped in all my days."

"I don't really care for your teasing," Saul shot back. Then he smiled. "I'm far from whipped but I'm mature enough not to pretend. I want Annie back."

"Mature? So that's what they're calling it now."

Saul waved him off and made his way to the steps. He ribbed, "Try not to eat me out of house and home before tomorrow morning. I'm going to bed."

Thursday couldn't come fast enough.

When Saul made his way downstairs, he heard a tune blasting and smiled at her humming. Annie was back.

He sniffed the air smelling cinnamon. French toast sticks. He licked his lips and said, "You're here."

He heard the volume lower and welcomed the sound of her sweet voice. "I couldn't sleep. Corey left. I tried to tell him to wait until you'd awakened before taking off, but he was confident you wouldn't mind. I hated just twiddling my thumbs so I started beating eggs…"

He smiled at her chatter. All was right in his world. "Corey was right. I gave him his severance and added a hefty bonus. Since you're making breakfast, I'll set the table."

"Show off," Annie said. "Let me turn the music up."

On impulse, he asked, "Can we move this outside? Even though I can't see the water, it's soothes me."

"What a great idea! The day is too beautiful to be cooped up inside. It's not that hot for July, so we should enjoy it." With quick speed, she was out the sliding glass door. Saul had done a good job with situating their plates on the patio table.

Saul appreciated the heat of the sun. He leaned back and sighed. He could get used to this—he and

Annie sharing relaxing moments out here together. For the first time, his life felt full and rich. He attributed a lot of that to the woman a mere two feet away from him.

As they dug into their meal, he didn't stall in addressing the issue uppermost on his mind. "Tell me why you abandoned me."

***

Annie coughed. He didn't even give her a chance to enjoy the meal. But that was Saul. He wouldn't be him if he sat back waiting on her to gather her courage. He owned three car dealerships and they flourished even through the economic downturn for a reason. Saul Sweeterman didn't sit back and wait for life to happen.

"I was scared." Three simple words filled with so much truth.

"Scared of what? Of me, of us, of what we're feeling?"

He fired the questions at her but Annie was quick on her feet. "Of all three," she countered. "Saul, there is something I need to share with you and I admit it's the main reason I ran. First, though, I apologize for leaving the way I did. It was an unprofessional act of cowardice."

"I accept your apology, but don't belabor the point. Get to why you left."

He was all business. Annie gathered her wits. It was obvious that Saul wasn't about to let her wiggle out of this conversation. She had to quit her stalling. But, talking about race wasn't easy, particularly when it could end a promising relationship.

She took a deep breath. "I realize you have feelings for me and I didn't want things to get too deep when you don't really know me. I may not look the way you imagine."

She saw his eyebrows furrow. "Do you think me so fickle that I wouldn't want you because of how you look? I touched your face. I know who are you on the inside. You're beautiful. You have a sharp wit. You make me laugh. It doesn't matter to me what you look like. I'm a man and real men want more than a beautiful face. We want a woman who'll stand by our side no matter what. We want women like you. No, let me make this personal. I don't just want any woman. I can get that. I. Want. You."

Annie felt tears dim her eyes. She knew he meant every word. She knew she was beautiful. Her parents had given her good genes. A former homecoming queen, Annie didn't need to hide her face under a paper bag. But, what she couldn't hide was her skin color.

Why don't you take him at his word?

Why bother telling him when he may never see again? What he doesn't know doesn't hurt, right?

As the thoughts raced through her mind, Annie remained silent. Saul must have thought she didn't believe him. In a swift move, he jumped to his feet and grabbed her with stunning accuracy. He pulled her close and buried his nose in her hair.

"Since you don't believe me, let me show you the only way I know how." He kissed the top of her head. "You smell so good. Like vanilla." His hands rifled through her curls. "A man could get lost in your thick, luscious curls."

Curls that were a product of her Native American lineage. *Stop him.* Annie told herself she needed to put the brakes on what was sure to be a successful seduction. She trembled at his touch. She'd savor the sensations rocking her body for just a minute. He kissed her neck. Then her ear. Okay, one more minute, then she would push him away. She felt his lips on her forehead. Another thirty seconds. Then he kissed both cheeks. He drew perilously close to her mouth.

All it took was a second; Saul took her upper lip into his mouth. She reacted by grabbing ahold of his hair. Her hands ploughed through the silky mane savoring his answering groan. *Whew! Lord, help me.* Okay, this had gone on long enough. She had to put an end to this madness.

She pushed her way out of his arms, and drew several deep breaths. She looked at Saul, recognizing the smile of male dominance. She wasn't always saved. She knew a satisfied man when she saw one.

"I'm guessing I proved my point," he said, basking in the moment. She appreciated his disheveled hair. It made him look…hot.

"No doubt about that," she purred. Okay, her voice was a dead giveaway. She cleared her throat. "You've more than made your point."

He strode into the house presumably to put some distance between them.

Well, he definitely deserved bragging rights because if she didn't have the Holy Spirit constraining her, they'd be finishing this 'conversation' in his bedroom. Scriptures flowed into her mind until her heart rate slowed to normal.

Her conscience rode her. Annie had ducked out of telling him the whole truth but she refused to dwell on it. She had told him in so many words. Still Saul insisted that he cared only about her inner beauty.

Annie's lips still tingled. She raised one hand to touch them, awed by the desire fanning her body. She was a grown woman. In seconds, she'd been reduced to a whimpering schoolgirl. She needed to flee from this temptation. How could she stay under his roof after that kiss?

She verbalized her thoughts as soon as he returned, looking more composed. "Maybe I should ask Corey to come back."

"You're going to drive me insane," Saul grunted. "I don't want Corey back. Listen, I'm not a Neanderthal. I'm capable of restraint. I'll keep my lips and hands to myself. I'll behave above board. I know you're trying to do right by God and I have no intention of messing with that. I can respect you enough to honor your commitment to God. That's what you do when you're in love."

Her breath caught. She sounded like the heroine in a cheap romance novel but Annie had to ask, "What did you say?"

"I said I respect your wishes because I'm in love with you."

"You love me?" she repeated the question with a voice that mirrored her confusion. "But, how can you love me when you've never seen me?"

"How can you ask me that when you're a Christian? You love Christ and you've never seen Him." She couldn't fault his reasoning.

"Yes, but—

"But nothing. I don't have to see you with my eyes. I just have to see you with my heart." He ambled over to her. She reached her hand out to help him determine her exact location. He faced her. His blue eyes reflected all of his pent-up emotion. "I love you, Annie Hays, so accept it. Don't question it. I love you."

"I love you, too," she said, finally believing and accepting. The words had been torn from her heart and poured from her mouth. She squashed any niggling doubts and concerns, convinced that with emotions as strong as his, he would overlook the color of her skin. Saul engulfed her into his arms and gave her a tight squeeze. Annie held on refusing to let go.

That's unrealistic mumbo-jumbo and you know it.

Prayer changes things, she countered.

A person has to want to change for change to happen.

At that point she closed her mind off to any warnings. If this isn't right, then I don't know what is.

Chapter Eighteen

Saul was going crazy. It had been thirty long days of tossing and turning all night thinking about her. He enjoyed their Bible study sessions and attended church with Annie every Sabbath. He enjoyed their walks now that his leg was as good as new. Both of them avoided that topic, as neither was ready for their idyllic situation to end. Boca Grande was reclusive and exclusive so they had spent lots of time getting to know each other. However, they knew it was time for her to go home. It had been difficult, but Saul had lived up to his word and kept his hands and lips off her.

Why had he made such a stupid promise? They were adults.

Saul had become very independent and things with Cassandra were progressing nicely. After his last visit with the eye doctor he'd heard more of the same. "Your eyes are physically fine. I've no idea why you're not able to see."

Blah blah blah. He was done with trying to figure that out. Saul appreciated the years he'd had his sight but how could he be depressed when Annie was so cheerful? She didn't seem to care that he couldn't see.

What Saul appreciated the most were her prayers. One morning his body was talking to him and he went and stood outside her door. Since she'd moved back into his home, Annie stayed in the bedroom that once belonged to Cassandra.

Saul had been about to knock when he heard sounds coming through her door. He pressed his ear to listen in and to his surprise she'd been praying for him. He heard her calling out his name to God asking Him for healing and deliverance. Saul leaned on the door with tears in his eyes.

He'd never known what it is what like to truly be loved until that moment. A woman who prayed for you with such fervor and consistency was one worth keeping. He walked away humbled beyond belief.

But, at nighttime, Saul struggled which was why he was gathering the courage to ask Annie to join him down by the beach. He knocked with more firmness than he realized. The door shot open.

"Are you all right?"

No. I'm in heat. "Yes, I just wanted to see if you would like to sit with me on the beach. The night is young."

"Give me five minutes to get changed."

As they sat on the beach clad in swimwear. Saul felt a pang. "I wish I could see you. You said you had brown eyes and hair. I'm thinking Sandra Bullock, or Kate Beckingsdale." He turned to ask, "Am I close?"

"Not even," she said. "Try Thandie Newton or Paula Patton."

"Hmmm… I don't think I know them."

"Why am I not surprised?"

Her wry tone made him defend himself. "Sorry if I'm out of the loop. I haven't had time to go to the movies and even then I'm not good with the remembering names."

He leaned into her and nuzzled her hair. "You smell like apricots."

"Hmm…" He felt her edging away from him and yanked his arm around her waist to still her movement. She wasn't going anywhere if he could help it. What he had planned required close proximity.

"I've been a man of my word, haven't I?" he prodded.

"Yes, you have."

"It's much more frustrating that I thought."

"Saul, you're dragging and that's not like you. Get to the point."

"I want to kiss you," he said. "I want to feel my lips pressed against yours."

"Oh, I want you to so bad, but I can't." Annie confessed. "If I kiss you, I might forget I'm a child of God and…I can't."

He wanted to make her forget but she sounded like she was really struggling. "Okay, no kissing, for now." He nibbled on her ear and kissed her on the cheek. "Hug me," he whispered.

She grabbed him tight. He felt the tip of her tongue touch his neck. Now he was confused. Wasn't this the same woman who lectured him minutes ago? He felt her hands in his hair and read the signs. Her body pretty much told the truth. Saul told himself that he'd sit and let her explore. If it killed him, he would help her keep her chastity.

***

"Saul, I want you but we've got to stop," she croaked while she dragged her hands through his hair.

He groaned but pulled away. Goose bumps rose on her flesh. She missed his nearness. She sat upright and brushed the sand out of her hair and dress. She'd donned a sarong over her bathing suit.

Saul sat as still as stone. Only his deep breaths kept Annie from wondering if he were alive. His face was unreadable.

Compelled, she spoke, "I—I wasn't trying to lead you on. Please don't be mad at me."

"I'm not."

The two words were torn from him. She touched him and he flinched. Surprised, she jerked her hand away. He was mad. Her thoughts raced. Annie grabbed her towel and stood.

What must Saul think of her? She felt guilty of that and the fact that she'd stretched the truth a wee bit earlier. The real reason she stopped the kiss was because Saul didn't know he would be locking lips with a sister. She needed to tell him the truth.

"Annie?"

Now. She needed to tell him now.

Annie looked at his face. "I'm here." She couldn't tell him. Not yet. Annie helped him to his feet and they made their way inside the house.

Troubled, she remained quiet most of the way. She wanted to retreat to her room to think but Saul wasn't having it.

"Watch a movie with me."

"Let's wash up and I'll meet you in the family room." It took her ten minutes to return. He was already there. She noted his curly wet hair and ached to run her hands through it again.

"Come snuggle with me," Saul suggested, having heard her entrance.

Annie complied and soon, they were engrossed in the story. At a pivotal scene, she turned to ask him a question, then sighed. To her dismay, he'd fallen asleep. She pressed the off-button on the remote and tried to move.

She was locked in. "Saul! Saul!" she gave a loud whisper. After several attempts, she released a deep breath. "I give up." Annie snuggled closer. Within minutes, she too was asleep.

"We spent our first night together," greeted her when she awoke to consciousness the next morning.

"What time is it? I expected to be up a long time ago! Why didn't you wake me? We'll be late to your last consultation with Dr. Pryor if we don't hurry." Annie peppered questions at him as she rolled up the blanket he must've placed on her while she slept.

"It's a little after nine," he answered. "Relax, there

was a cancellation so I was able to secure a later time. We go in at eleven."

They made it to Fawcett with minutes to spare. Saul insisted on stopping at Abbe's Donuts first. It took every ounce of patience she possessed to accommodate him. She tugged on her jeans, having forgotten her belt, and raced through the door with Saul in tow.

Today was the day they'd find out if he'd been cleared of physical therapy. It took a half-hour for Saul to be x-rayed and another ten minutes passed before the doctor arrived.

Dr. Pryor ushered them into his office. "I'll make this quick. Saul, your scans look good. Unless you have any residual concerns, I'm officially clearing you for all physical activities. Your bones have healed as they should and I'm happy to say this is your last visit with me, and your last session with Annie." He faced her with a wide smile. "I for one am glad for that. Annie, your presence has been missed. Can't wait to get you back into rotation." With that, he left the room.

Saul gathered his cane and stood. "Wow."

One word. How eloquent. Annie wiped a tear from her face. "I'm so happy for you. Not all cases have such a promising end. You must be relieved."

"I am—it's just a lot to process."

Their gait was slow as they departed the ward and headed towards the elevator. Annie waved at some of the nurses and fellow therapists. Sari wasn't on duty until the afternoon.

"It's been such a pleasure working with you, Saul." She gulped through her 'exit' speech. He came to an abrupt halt at her words.

"What do you mean?"

Annie didn't answer until they were ensconced in the car. She took U.S. and drove to make the left at El Jobean. "You know what the clearance means. I'll be packing my bags and returning home. You'll still work with your vision and mobility specialist for years to come, but you don't need me anymore." She injected professional enthusiasm as she tried to cover her sniffles.

"Are you crying?" he asked. "Listen, stop those tears. I've no intention of you going anywhere. You belong with me. I make enough money to support you so you have no worries."

"What kind of nonsense talk is that?" she hurled at him. "I'm going home. I'm not going to shack up with you. My God won't allow it. Do you want your other leg broken?"

Saul didn't bat an eyelash. "I wasn't talking about us shacking up, as you put it. I was talking about you becoming—

She cut him off. She spoke through her teeth. "Don't you dare say what I think you're about to say! I'm driving and concentrating on the road. Listen, don't say another word until we're back home." She realized her mistake and corrected. "I mean back at your home." Annie really wasn't that mad but she had to stall him.

"Fine, I can wait," Saul replied with ill-concealed annoyance. He muttered, "Imagine, the second woman I ever think of asking to marry me cuts me off."

Annie rolled her eyes when she saw he was sulking. Well let him sit and stew. Better that, than deal with her real problem. She didn't care where he asked her to marry him, as long as he did. She had to talk to him first. He had to know the truth.

She tensed imagining his reaction. She couldn't get to his house fast enough. Great. There was traffic ahead. She decelerated. She tilted her head to look ahead. "There's an accident ahead," she explained to Saul. Her patience was wearing thin and she emitted a loud growl.

He placed his left hand on her lap and patted. "Keep cool. We're in no rush."

Warmth crept up her spine and Annie blurted, "I love you."

"I love you, too. Even when you're crazy."

She inched the car by the scene. Like most of the drivers she turned her head with curiosity. The mangled heap in front of her made her heart leap. "Lord, have mercy on whoever was driving that car."

Wait a minute…

No! No! She prayed she was wrong. She rolled her window down to get a closer look. She had to make sure before she opened her mouth. She saw the blond hair and the telltale car jewelry. She knew who owned that car!

She grabbed Saul's hand. "That's Cassandra's car!"

Chapter Nineteen

Two accidents in a matter of months. Saul grabbed his forehead. "I'm too old for this. I'm getting you a Hummer. You need something indestructible."

"Too old for what, Grandpa?" Emily piped up. She looked up from her iPad where she'd been coloring to ask the question. "If you weren't old then you wouldn't be a grandpa."

In spite of his situation, he couldn't help but laugh at her reasoning. He grazed the stubble on his chin.

"She makes you sound ancient," Cassandra remarked from her hospital bed. Her throat sounded hoarse from being poked and prodded.

Saul looked towards his daughter and smiled. He couldn't stem the words bursting from his being. "I'm so relieved. I could be crying now. Instead, I'm rejoicing. A part of me wants to find that fool mechanic and wrap my hands around his neck, but a greater part of me is too busy following Annie and thanking God that you're alive. I mean who forgets to tighten the lug nuts on four tires?" Anger rose within him.

Her voice caught. "When the tires loosened, and I

felt the car drop, my heart gave out. All I could think about was Emily in the rear seat. I screamed but as Annie said, God helped me. I would've gone home but I'm here at your insistence."

"The airbag deployed. I wanted you both checked out completely just to make sure." Saul looked upwards. "I could've lost my daughter and granddaughter twice." Suddenly the weight of the past several months bore down on him and Saul cried. He wailed as the enormity of his experiences pierced his heart. He knew without a doubt that his survival had been a miracle, evidence of a very real God. Annie had pointed that out to him several times but he was just getting it. Who was he that the Creator of the world had interceded on his behalf so many times?

"I'll be back," he urged, not wanting Emily to see him break down. He stood outside the door and sobbed quietly. He felt someone touch his arm and then a friendly voice.

"I'm a nurse. Can I help you?"

"Yes, can you take me to the chapel?"

The nurse led him to the elevator and down to the lobby where the chapel was located. Saul thanked her and asked, "Can you let my daughter know where I am? I was standing outside her door when you found me."

He felt a light pat on his shoulder. "Yes, I'll do that," she said before leaving him alone.

He heard the door click shut. Glad to be alone, he spoke. "God, I don't have much to say because I'm not usually a praying man. I just wanted to tell You thank You for sparing my daughter's life today—and, my granddaughter." He gulped.

Saul tilted his head. "God, are you hearing me?" His voice echoed.

"This is silly," Saul said, laughing at himself. "It's not like I expect You to answer. Although Annie says You hear prayers and answer them."

He cleared his throat. Better get back to his prayer. He closed his eyes. "I also want to thank You for bringing Annie into my life. She's been good for me. I've been learning a lot about You from her." Even though he was alone, Saul lowered his voice before continuing. "I might as well tell you that I love Annie and I plan to ask her to marry me."

Chapter Twenty

Annie peeked in on Cassandra. In her hand, she held a fast food bag with a hamburger and fries for Emily to eat. Cassandra gave her a grateful look. After she was ensured that they were all right, Annie had left to give Saul time with his family.

"You're so good with her. I know what my Dad sees in you. Do you have children?"

"No, not yet. I had hoped to have one or two before I turned forty but at this rate...Where's your father by the way?"

"A nurse told me he's in the chapel," Cassandra said. "I want to thank you. Because of you, my father and I have a relationship again and he is Emily's favorite person in the world."

"I didn't do anything," Annie said, lowering her head, slightly embarrassed by the young woman's effusive gratitude. She covered her cheeks. "You're making me blush from your praise."

"You deserve it," the younger woman insisted. "Daddy is changing because of you. He's talking about God and he's so happy with you. I'm begging you to forgive me for how I greeted you when we first met."

Annie squirmed with recollection. "It's old news," she said, hoping Cassandra wouldn't continue the conversation strain.

"No, I can't let it go. I mean I was insulting and I'm ashamed of my behavior. I should've never come at you like that about your race. I mean, I'm a fine one to talk."

She felt ill at ease. "Cassandra, consider it forgotten, although I expected you to tell your father. However, my motives were selfish because then I wouldn't be stuck with the task. I never thought twice of our difference in race because this town is filled with interracial couples. I was going to tell him today but this trumped my confession. Now I'm afraid that your father will be furious and think I was keeping this from him on purpose."

Cassandra gave Annie a curious look. "Why didn't you tell him sooner?"

"I'm scared to death he'll reject me. I want him to see me and love me as a person—a woman. I don't want to lose him."

"I'm going to be blunt. You were dead wrong to wait this long."

Annie closed her eyes and accepted full blame. "I'll tell him, tonight. The nurse told me they're working on your discharge papers so once we drop you off at your home, I'll come clean."

"I'll give you a couple of days. If you don't, I will. Daddy needs the truth. You can't build love with a lie as the foundation."

Saul entered the room within seconds of Cassandra's warning, ending the conversation. Annie had been half-afraid that he'd overhead, but he was in good spirits.

***

As she pulled into the driveway, Annie was solemn. Saul stirred awake. They entered his home. She turned on the interior lights, feeling drained.

"What a day filled with highs and lows," Saul declared, mirroring her thoughts.

She brushed past him. "I have to talk to you and I can only hope it ends on a high."

"Is someone dying?" he asked.

"No."

"Well, it can't be that bad."

He reached for her. Annie took his hand and allowed him to pull her into his comforting embrace. Saul led her to the loveseat and massaged her temples. She bit back a moan. He placed his lips on her eyelids. Then he kissed the bridge of her nose. "Annie, I love you. Will you marry me?"

Her heart skipped a beat and she inhaled. Yes, she wanted to marry him. However she opened her mouth and gave the only answer she could. "I can't."

He pulled away.

Annie twisted her hands. The air between them dropped to point of frosty. *Lord, give me courage.*

While she prayed, Saul reached for her hand. "Why can't you marry me? Is there a boyfriend that I don't know about?"

If only it were that easy, Annie thought. She removed her hands from his and placed them in her lap. "No, there is no boyfriend. Saul, I haven't been honest with you. There's something you need to know."

"Annie, just spit it. I'm losing patience."

With a slight shiver, Annie began, "The day I met Cassandra she told me that her husband was black. She told me you were against her marrying a black man. When she married Kellan, you ended your relationship with her."

Saul hung his head. "Yes, that's true. It wasn't one of my proudest moments. But, we've patched things up since then." He shook his head. "I fail to see what this has to do with you marrying me."

Annie looked at his creased brows. She took a deep breath before she said, "I have a problem with that because I'm black."

"Wh…What?"

"I said I'm—

"I heard what you said."

Looking at him, Annie couldn't gauge his reaction. His lips were scrunching and he fumed, taking shallow breaths.

"That's why I ran," she said. "I ran from my feelings but I was wrong. God led me back to you."

"Don't bring God into this. Because I can't see Him condoning being lied to and made a fool of" Saul spat. He gave a chuckle filled with self-recrimination. "Cassie must've had a field day watching me lose my head over a black woman. No wonder she didn't say anything. She was having a laugh at my expense."

Annie rushed to take his hand. "No, she wasn't. I promise you that. She urged me to tell you truth."

He pushed her hand away and cut in. "So, if my daughter didn't tell you to confess you would've kept me in the dark about something this important."

He was turning her words against her. Her body shivered under his accusation.

"No … I … I had every intention of telling you … but …"

"But, nothing!" he yelled. He stood. "Annie, I appreciate everything you've done for me but leave my house."

No. He can't be ending things. "You told me you loved me."

"That was before," he snarled.

"Before I told you I was black?" she grounded out with clenched fists.

"No, before you lied to me! Now get out!" he screamed.

Chapter Twenty-One

The pounding on the door jarred him awake. "Go away!" Saul moaned. Whoever it was refused to leave. He swung his legs out of bed and reached for his cane. With sure steps, he made his way towards the front door.

He swung the door open.

"It's about time you answered the door." Cassandra sounded put out with him. "I've been ringing the bell for about five minutes."

He felt a tug on his cane. It had to be Emily. She liked to hold onto it. Saul ignored Cassandra who was still busy with her tirade. He ignored her comments about his haggard appearance. He squatted and held his arms out, bracing his body for the impact.

"Grandpa!" Emily greeted as she sprinkled his face with kisses. "Ugh! Your breath, Grandpa!"

Saul couldn't hold the chuckle. He knew he hadn't kept up with his hygiene. He stood and hurried into his bathroom to brush his teeth. Wetting his hands, he ran his fingers through his hair. He rubbed his chin. He'd shaved later. His orientation and mobility trainer, Beth

Williams had taught him how to do it almost as good as when he had his sight.

"Why aren't you answering my calls? I've been trying to reach you for two weeks." Cassie didn't wait for his response. "Where's Annie?" she asked.

"She's gone." Saul faced her general direction. He hoped his face didn't show his pain. He missed her. He was angry, yes. But, he missed her.

"Gone?" Cassandra repeated. "No wonder you look like crap."

Saul shook his head. "I'm fine," he lied. Then he purposely injected a light tone. "So I bet you had a good laugh about me going crazy for a black woman."

"Oh, she told you."

"Yes, she did."

"And, you ran her off? I know you can't see me, but my mouth is hanging open. Why would you do that?" He heard the incredulity in Cassie's voice.

"She lied to me," he said. Only to himself, would he admit that his excuse was weak. This was about race. Nothing else.

"How did she lie?" Cassie demanded.

"She should've told me."

"Yes, and she did," his daughter said. "Dad, this is about race."

He jutted his chin. "It just isn't done." He tapped his cane on the floor to signify he was done with the discussion.

"Says who?"

Before he could answer, Emily interrupted. "Mommy, I need to go bathroom."

"Okay, honey," he heard her reply. "You know where it is."

He heard Emily race across the tile as she went to relieve herself.

"Says who?" Cassandra repeated.

Saul shifted. He navigated his way to the breakfast barstool and sat. He heard Cassie open the refrigerator. "Want cereal?" she asked.

Saul nodded. "Says my father and my grandfather and my great grandfather. It's understood."

"Dad, that's way past stupid. It's ignorant. So, you'd rather remain alone than be glad you've found love again?"

Saul smiled. "I did, didn't I? I thought your mother was it for me. Then I met Annie ... and ..." he stopped. And what?

When she placed the cereal box before him, Saul heard the contents rattle. "Need help?" she asked. Her voice held displeasure at his answer. He knew she wasn't done.

"No, I can do it," he said with a small smile. He'd come a long way.

He reached out to touch it so he would know its location. Saul heard the clink of the bowl and held out his hand until he felt the cool metal in his hand.

He placed the spoon on the right of his bowl and

opened the cereal box. Then he placed his finger in the bowl and poured so he would know when to stop.

"The milk is on your left."

"It's for the best. Things would be too complicated," Saul said, returning to the conversation of he and Annie.

Saul found the milk bottle, undid the cap and poured the milk using the same technique. By then, Emily had returned and asked for some cereal.

Cassie helped her out before she said, "Dad, with all due respect, that's the dumbest thing I've ever heard."

Saul arched a brow but said nothing.

"You love her. Are you telling me that's changed because of her color?"

He slumped a little. No, his feelings hadn't changed. "I love her," he admitted between bites. "But I'm angry."

"She can't help her skin color any more than you can help who you love!" Cassie bellowed. Then she continued in a calmer tone, "I don't know what stereotypes you have about blacks, but Kellan was a good, decent husband. I feel the pain of losing him every day and I'm angry that he's gone!"

Her heartfelt outcry pulled at his heart. "Like you, I'm angry. But not at Annie, like I believed. I'm angry at myself," Saul admitted.

"I might be angry, However, I have no regrets. I'm glad to have had Kellan in my life even if our forever was cut short," Cassie clarified.

"Are you saying things were easy for the both of you?" Saul asked.

"No, it wasn't easy. Sometimes, we'd go into Wal-Mart or the movie theater and we'd get these bad looks. Sometimes, we'd have people say some mean things because we were together. But, we were together. We loved each other and that's what mattered."

Cassie's words pierced his being. Saul hung his head. She was right. He called out. "Come over here and take my hand." When she did, he said, "I'm proud of you. I'm glad you stood up to me and went with your heart."

He heard a sniff before she rested her head on his shoulder. Saul tensed. She used to do the same thing when she was a little girl. He got choked up. "I'm sorry I wasn't there with you."

She nodded. "It's okay. I had Kellan."

He nodded. "In a way, I'm glad I'm blind because I don't think I would've taken the chance to truly see people otherwise. I was so caught up with race that I forgot we're all human."

He heard Cassie's indrawn breath. "What are you saying?"

"I made a mistake. I shouldn't have let Annie go. I made a mess of things. I allowed my pride and anger to push her away." He slumped. "It's too late."

Cassie stepped away from him and cleared his now empty breakfast bowl. He heard her put the items away.

"She won't want me now," Saul voiced.

"She fell in love with you knowing how you felt,"

Cassie said. "I don't think a love like that just dissipates into thin air. Go to her, Dad. Grovel. Beg. Do whatever you have to, but don't let love pass you by without a fight."

Chapter Twenty-Two

"Call him, already!" Sari demanded, "Because I can't take anymore of your moping. Not even when Cornell left did you walk around like somebody died."

"Why are you in here?" Annie demanded. She bent closer to her bathroom mirror to inspect the bags under her eyes. Too many sleepless nights were catching up to her.

"You're avoiding me," Sari explained as she covered the doorway. "So now I've got you cornered."

Annie rolled her eyes and pushed past her. "It's six o'clock in the morning. I'm not avoiding you. I've been helping you plan a wedding. Remember? There's nothing else to talk about with Saul. I told you he kicked me out of his house. What else is there to discuss?"

"Normally, I would be high-fiving you for leaving. But you're miserable! I know he has a temper but how do you know he's not regretting the way he handled things? There's only one way to find out. I'm saying put your pride on the line and go see him," her friend entreated.

She brushed her teeth and rinsed them while she thought. Sari wouldn't move. Annie knew she was waiting for answer. She wiped her hands and turned to face the other woman. "It's not my pride that's on the line. It's my heart."

Sari's eyebrows creased with empathy. "I know that and if he were in a position to come here, I would tell you to wait for him to come crawling back. But, you blocked his number. His only means of reaching you."

Annie nodded. That she had. She crossed her arms. "That's what he gets for kicking me out of his house."

Sari's mouth formed an 'O'. "I see. You're punishing him. Not cool. I get it, but I can't agree." Her friend exited the bathroom.

"You've changed," Annie accused following after her. "You wouldn't take such behavior from Ahmad."

"No, I wouldn't. However, that's when I would count on my friend to tell me to fix things. I'd count on you to tell me that you can't tell your heart who to love."

Sari sure was right about that, Annie thought. She'd tried to tell her heart whom not to love and it wasn't cooperating. Annie yearned to see Saul. She'd cried every night despite her prayers. She dreamt about him. She knew God was urging her not to give up on him. He was still working on Saul.

"I'm afraid of his rejection," she whispered. Her lips quivered with her words.

Sari pulled her in for a hug. "I know that. Seeing your pain made me pray long and hard about this as well. I'm urging you to quit spiting yourself and go to him. I believe in my spirit, he's the one for you."

"He doesn't deserve a second chance."

"True, but who does? Nothing good comes easy. Especially not relationships." Sari raised an eyebrow. "I should know."

Tears fell. Sari's words were sinking in but she had a ways to go. "Pray with me."

Sari beckoned for them to join hands. "Okay, I will, but you've got to return the favor and pray for Saul. Because of you, he may have a different perspective of love. He fell in love with you. Now, show him the perspective of a Christian. Show him God's love by forgiving him."

They bowed their heads and Sari prayed.

When they opened their eyes, Annie said, "I know it's a bit dramatic, but I feel like Esther. I'm going back there not knowing if I will be allowed in."

Sari chuckled at her comparison. "It is a tad dramatic." She patted Annie's arm. "He loves you. He'll let you in."

In the face of Sari's quiet conviction, Annie dressed. Within fifteen minutes, she was behind the wheel. Her sweaty palms gripped the wheel. She was either about to find her destiny, or meet her doom.

Chapter Twenty-Three

Saul pushed open the door to his lanai and sniffed the air. He smelled the ocean and savored the feel of the crisp morning air. He inhaled. He smelled coffee and that signature light floral scent, which could only mean one thing.

"Macy? What are you doing here?"

"Saul, I couldn't let you go."

Right words. Wrong woman. He heard the words coming out of Macy's lips and couldn't help but think, *If only it was Annie saying these words.*

Macy must have entered the night before using his spare key. What happened to her being gone? He turned towards her to ask the question uppermost on his mind.

"Macy, why are you here?" He hadn't brought his cane; comfortable enough now in his own home to do without it at times. He reached a hand out to feel for the patio chair and lowered himself into it.

She deflected his question by offering him coffee. "I made you a cup. I knew you'd be up soon."

He could tell by her voice that she was smiling. He was an early riser. It was just a little past six-thirty a.m.

Saul curled his hands around the cup liking the warmth. He took a long sip liking the feel of the steaming heat that hit his face. Macy always made good coffee.

Come to think of it, there were so many great qualities about her.

"I'm here because I know I said we were over but in my heart I can't let you go that easy. I barely made it through my photo shoot. As I stood there doing pose after pose, all I could think of was you."

Her loud sniff alerted him to the fact that she was crying. Concerned, he placed his mug on the table and reached out across the table to hold her hand.

"I ... I ... I know you may not love me the way I love you, but we used to be friends. I miss our friendship. You used to be so perfect. I miss the old you before you were—

She stopped. Saul knew she was searching for a tactful word. "Blind?" he filled in. "That's the problem right there. I'm blind. This is the new me. Blindness is my new world and I'm learning how to live with it."

He knew it would hurt, but he had to tell her the truth. "I know you love me, but you're not a part of my new world."

Judging by her harsh intake of breath, he knew his words stung. He squirmed in his seat but he meant the words.

"I want to be, but you won't let me in," she said.

"You would mother me," he explained. "I don't need to be coddled like I'm helpless. I need to be independent."

"I can do that," Macy protested.

Saul shook his head. "Macy, I may never regain my sight. Can you live with that?"

"Don't say that. Your vision will return and things will go back to normal." He heard the slight hesitation in her voice.

"You're surrounded by perfection. I don't think you'd be able to deal with someone who's less than perfect."

"I'm not that shallow," she protested. "I love you just the way you are and I'll prove it."

The chair scraped. Her heels clicked on the floor. Saul moved his head tracking the sound. She was coming over to him.

He wasn't prepared for Macy to jump into his lap. With a small groan, she pressed her lips to his.

He heard a harsh intake of breath. Saul opened his eyes, jumped to his feet, dumping Macy off his lap.

He knew who that was. His head whipped around. *"Annie!"*

***

Annie froze. She should have rung the doorbell. Instead, knowing Saul's routine, she'd walked around the perimeter of the house to the lanai.

On her drive over, she'd prepared herself to hear "Get out!" She wasn't prepared to see Macy's lips pressed against Saul. From her vantage point, he was a willing participant.

"I've been praying and God... Sari said she... I thought..." She spun on her heels. *Stupid! Stupid! Stupid!*

She heard Macy calling out her name and broke into a run. The supermodel was the last person she wanted to talk to at the moment. However, she was no match for the other woman. Macy caught up to her before she made it to her car.

"Annie! Wait!" Macy grabbed her hand. "Saul almost broke his toe coming after you. He didn't have his cane."

Annie pursed her lips. She knew it wasn't Christ-like but she didn't care about his toe. It should've been his face. The same face that had been front-and-center in her dreams.

"What you saw—my kissing him—was a last ditch effort to salvage what we had. You wouldn't know it, but he wasn't responding. He was humoring me. I'm sure we'll still be friends. But, we're over."

Annie saw the other woman's face turn beet red.

She believed her. No woman would lie about that humiliation. Especially not one of the most beautiful women in the world. "Why? Why was he humoring you?"

Macy shook her head. "If I have to spell it out..." The other woman walked away leaving Annie to stew with her thoughts.

She stood there for several minutes. She heard Saul yelling her name. He called and called, but fear and unbelief kept her rooted to the spot.

Annie had come to him and she'd gotten an eyeful.

No. She wasn't going in.

She didn't care that she'd driven all this way.

If he wanted her, he'd have to come to her.

Decision made, Annie went back to her car. "Choose me. Come to me," she said as she backed out of the driveway.

Chapter Twenty-Four

Stop staring at him. Annie scolded herself.

But try as she might, she couldn't keep her eyes from straying to Saul. Dressed in his made-to-fit black suit, he'd attracted the eyes of many women in the congregation—even the married ones. Three days had passed since "the incident" as she phrased it. Annie had accepted Macy's explanation.

Now seeing Saul here in church, she couldn't keep the stupid grin off her face, either. He had come. He had come to her. Thank God.

People were going to think she was daft if she didn't quit with the never-ending smile. Annie watched him enter with Cassandra and Emily. The three sat together a few rows from the front.

"Sister Hays... Sister Aniyah Hays...I don't know where your attention is but it's time to come back to the present."

Annie jumped when she realized all eyes were on her. Laughter erupted as her hands covered her face with embarrassment. She looked towards the media crew and gave a slight nod. Tamela Mann's Take me to the King rang through the sanctuary. She lifted her arms and began to worship God with a praise dance. She rejoiced and worshiped and welcomed the "Hallelujahs" and "Amens". It meant God was in the place.

She was moved by the words. Her body echoed the sentiment when she ended her routine with a dramatic flourish on her knees. There wasn't a dry eye in the place.

In the midst of the rejoicing, Annie departed to change out of her praise and worship dance dress.

When she returned to her post in the choir, Pastor Charleston was at the podium. "Sister Hays, you're a vision. Angels in heaven couldn't do better." She nodded and smiled at the applause. She was so glad that God was glorified through her movement.

From her seat, she bowed her head to have a heartfelt talk to God. She whispered to Him from her heart. "Thank You, Lord for using me. I so wish Saul would've been able to see me. Holy Father, I thank You for how You've brought him this far. I thank You for Your healing in his life. I thank You that You changed his heart and that You've united him with his family. Lord, You're a deliverer and as You delivered the Hebrew boys and Daniel, I know this is nothing for You. I ask You to perform a miracle and restore his sight."

When she opened her eyes, Pastor Charleston had already begun his word. Her eyes widened. Of all things, he was talking about Saul.

***

Did he just hear his name?

Saul straightened. Yes, he did. The pastor was talking about a Biblical character that shared his name.

"Saul was zealous, but stubborn and set in his ways. When he made up his mind, nobody could make him budge." Pastor Charleston said. The congregation chuckled.

He felt a pinch on his arm and turned to his daughter. "He sounds like someone I know," she teased.

Saul gave her a slanted look, but didn't respond.

"Saul was on his way to Damascus road when something unexpected happened. He had a personal encounter with Jesus, which left him blind. Sometimes God is trying to reach us and steer us on the right path, but we refuse to heed. Saints, sometimes God has to blind us because we refuse to see."

"He's blind. Did you hear that?" Cassandra whispered.

He nodded. His heart pounded. He couldn't ignore the similarities. He and Saul shared a name. They'd both lost their sight. It was eerie, uncanny, and couldn't be mere coincidence.

Pastor Charleston continued, "Imagine losing your sight and having to rely on someone to lead and guide you. Can you imagine that scary feeling? You were once living and loving the light, but now all you see is nothing. You're surrounded by darkness and you don't know which way to turn."

Yes! Yes! He *knew* that feeling. He lived it. Experienced it everyday. Saul hunched over. He inhaled deeply. *Breathe easy. Breathe easy.* He exhaled. He felt Cassandra's hand on his arm and cupped her hand.

"Goodness. How does he know?" he asked, tortured. The morning he woke up realizing he saw nothing came back to him with full force. He'd been terrified. Alone. *Ugh!* He clenched his stomach. Remembering.

"Why did this happen to me? Saul wondered. He'd been stopped cold in his tracks. He had his own plan and he was all right with it. He could continue that way forever. But, God had a different plan for his life. He knew Saul was more than what he portrayed, but Saul had to see himself. There is a moment in a man's life when he has to see the wicked, awful being that he is." Pastor Charleston's words pierced him without mercy.

Others in the crowd started calling out, "Have mercy, Lord."

Yes, he'd been all right with disowning his daughter and rejecting his son-in-law and grandchild. Oh, how could he have done that? He covered his mouth, convulsing as tears fell. He was seeing himself clearly, and he didn't like how he looked. He swiped at the tears.

"Do you need to leave?" Cassandra's tone sounded worried.

He patted her on her leg and shook his head. "I can't leave. I'm all right."

Someone sat next to him and took his hand. Saul was pulled into a hug by a woman with ample-sized breasts. He smelled cocoa butter.

"That's it, let God talk to you," the woman said.

Saul nodded as he rocked back and forth. He was feeling the heat of God's spotlight.

"For three days, he stayed in this state, tortured and lost. But, God had a plan! God had a plan of respite. He had also made provision for Saul's deliverance by preparing a prophet. A man called Ananias."

Ananias. Annie Hays, or as he heard today, *Aniyah Hays. Oh. My. Lord.* Saul heard a harsh intake of breath. Cassandra hadn't missed the similarities between the names, either. Goose bumps rose.

"God commanded Ananias to pray for Saul and when he did, Saul's sight was restored. From that day until his death, Saul walked with God. Today, I urge you to walk with God. Come out of your seat. Come meet God at the altar."

He heard the music begin and the words, "All to Jesus, I surrender..." Saul sprang to his feet. Cassandra took his arm. It was time.

He was going to meet God.

With each step, Saul's confidence grew. He'd never been more sure of anything in his life—besides, Annie. He felt her presence next to him and welcomed her comforting touch.

Saul poured out his heart and accepted the beauty of God's forgiveness.

He opened his eyes. "Ugh! Arrgh!!" Saul screamed and rubbed his eyes. The brightness was too much and he covered them unsure of how to cope. He flailed through the crowd like a madman. Then he heard her voice. Annie. She was talking to him.

"Saul, it's okay. Accept it," she said. "Accept your miracle. Give your eyes a chance to adjust. Baby, you're healed!"

Saul calmed. He focused his eyes until he saw her. Beautiful Annie, standing there with tears streaming down her face. She held her hands out towards him. Saul raced towards her. "I can see! I can see!"

She nodded, "You can!"

The crowd went wild rejoicing and praising God, but Saul didn't care. His eyes were centered on the woman in front of him. He could barely believe what he was seeing. She was gorgeous. *Movie star* gorgeous. How'd he luck out like this! Hysterical, he laughed and clapped his hands with glee.

Annie's face shone as she laughed with him. But concern surfaced at his uncontrolled emotions. "Saul, honey… Are you okay?"

He gazed into her face and exclaimed, "You're the most beautiful woman I've ever seen! You didn't tell me you looked like this!"

All through the benediction, Saul rejoiced. "Isn't she stunning?" he would tap someone to say. "She's going to marry *me!*" he told someone else as he pointed towards her. Oh! That reminded him. Saul dug into his pockets and withdrew a small ring box. He skittered over to Annie and took her hand.

A beautiful red glow splashed across her cheeks. How intriguing. He needed to make her blush more often. With a booming voice, he asked, "Aniyah Hays, I know I was wrong about a lot of things, but I'm right about how I feel about you. I love you. I want to spend the rest of my life with you. Will you marry me?" He didn't wait for an answer before shoving the solitaire on her finger.

"You already know the answer," Annie smiled through teary eyes.

Saul dragged her outside the church and behind the parking lot. The sun burned his eyes but he was a man on a mission. What he intended to do wasn't suitable for inside God's house.

"I feel like a princess!" Annie said. "I'm entering my happy-ever-after."

"Yes you are, and there's only one way to end this fairytale," Saul agreed, as he gave his woman the kiss of true love.

Reader Guide Questions

- Do you think it is possible for a person to decide whom to love based on preferences, or does the heart decide? Why or why not?

- Was Saul prejudiced or just misguided?

- How are the characters and events outlined in the story similar to the life of Saul and Ananias?

- Do you think Annie should have ran away when she learned about Saul's position on interracial dating? Why or why not? If you were in her shoes, what do you think you would do?

- When Annie sees Macy and Saul kissing, she decides against confronting him. Did you agree with her decision? Why or why not?

- How do you feel about interracial dating? Have you or would you date outside your race? What are your biggest challenges, if any? Share your thoughts, opinions and experiences.

- There are people who state, "I don't look at color." Is it the notion of being "Color Blind" a possibility, or is it an ideal?

About the Author

Michelle Lindo-Rice enjoys crafting women's fiction with themes centered around the four "F" words: Faith, Friendship, Family and Forgiveness. Her first published work, Sing A New Song, was a Black Expressions featured selection. Originally from Jamaica West Indies, Michelle Lindo-Rice calls herself a lifelong learner.

She has earned degrees from New York University, SUNY at Stony Brook, and Teachers College, Columbia University. When she moved to Florida, she enrolled in Argosy University where she completed her Education Specialist degree in Education Leadership. A pastor's kid, Michelle upholds the faith, preaching, teaching and ministering through praise and worship.

You can connect with Michelle online at Facebook, LinkedIn, Google+, Twitter @mlindorice, or PLEASE join her mailing list at www.michellelindorice.com

Her blog: http://www.michellelindorice.blogspot.com

Read some of her other works:

Sing A New Song

Walk A Straight Line

My Steps Are Ordered

Printed in the USA
CPSIA information can be obtained
at www.ICGtesting.com
LVHW052102040923
757128LV00032B/300

9 781499 529616